The Twins

Alicia Freys

Contents

Chapter 1

The Riley twins were born in the spring of 1797 during a ferocious storm that battered the Salisbury Plain for three days together.

Isabel Riley entered the world with a flash of lightning, her shrieking drowned out by a grand clap of thunder. Thirteen minutes later the storm abated, clouds parted, and Miranda Riley was handed to her father, blinking in rays of sun that poured through the window.

Their mother joined the Lord's legion of angels less than an hour later. Lord Robin Augustus Riley, a nobleman of considerable wealth, was left to raise his new twin daughters alone at the ripe age of thirty; though not entirely alone, for his brother-in-law and sister (Mr and Mrs Lawrence) immediately took themselves and their children (six-year-old Edwin and eight-month-old Charity) to Tenby Hall to assist him in his grief. Mrs Lawrence took great pains in hiring a governess for the children and spent her every waking moment with her nieces for the first three months of their life; and visited (with her family) for two months of every summer thereafter.

Lord Riley also had two very good friends in his neighbors, Lord and Lady Westbrook and their son. The Westbrook's were the wealthier of the two families, making fourteen thousand a year to the Riley's ten thousand. They were as close as family; thus, the Westbrooks mourned with Lord Riley in equal measure.

Six years passed and the pain faded, replaced with happy memories; but life is not often content with only a little tragedy and a grave illness struck Thornhill Manor, the Westbrook's home. Seventeen-year-old Matthew was removed to the Riley's home lest he also become ill, while his parents – along with half of Thornhill's staff – suffered until death. This time, Mr Lawrence came to the rescue (along with his wife and children) and lingered at Tenby Hall for nearly a year while he and Lord Riley aided young Lord Matthew Westbrook in managing his newly inherited estate and holdings. Matthew Westbrook and Edwin Lawrence became fast friends despite the difference in their ages.

Miranda and Isabel knew not grief. They knew they had no mama but it affected them little. They were saddened by the passing of Lord and Lady Westbrook, but being only six years of age did not fully understand death nor miss their family friends for very long. As they grew older, they had fond and fleeting memories of the couple they had considered a second papa and mama, and loved young Mr Westbrook as if he were their brother.

The lives of Miranda and Isabel were full of luxury, love, and joy. They were adorned in silks, velvets, jewels, and pearls; given playthings, and ponies, and delicacies such as chocolates and sweets; they giggled and played together during the dinner parties and glittering balls held in their opulent home and, on occasion, at the grand Thornhill Manor; peaking down from the higher levels on the swirling couples below and dancing together as their governess clapped and told them they were the most splendid dancers she had ever seen.

Garden parties in the summer were their favorite, for they loved the out-doors; and that was when it was easiest to travel so garden parties usually offered a generous number of young friends to play with as well.

"It is a marvel how two children can be so alike, yet at the same time so different!" Their Aunt Lizzie observed as she sat with a group of ladies during one of these garden parties. They were currently watching the two girls – who were, at this time, eight years of age – play in the shade of the garden trees. Miranda sat with two other girls her age, pale-blond waves almost glittering in the rays of sun that escaped through the leaves; she was giggling with her friends as they made little bouquets of wildflowers with help from their father and Mr Westbrook. Miranda was jumping for a low-hanging branch of apple blossoms.

"Here Em. Let me get that for you." Westbrook used the family's pet name for the child as he plucked a sprig of apple blossoms from the branch and handed them down to her.

"Thank you." She enunciated carefully, focused on stuffing the blooms into her cluster of grass and buttercups with such concentration, face so serious, that Westbrook and Lord Riley chuckled at her. A shout caused them to look towards where Isabel was playing with a group of boys their age.

Izzy brandished a stick – a shining golden sword in the eyes of she and her companions – and rallied her troops, ashy-blond curls constrained in long ribbons. "Aye men, to me! We gotta get those Pirates!"

One boy asked tentatively "Do you think I could be captain now? You've been captain most the whole time."

"You can't just get given captaincy Eugene." Izzy stated disdainfully, "You need fight for it. Or.." A sparkle entered her big grey eyes "There is a way you can be a captain with me."

"What way." Eugene Dunsworth asked warily.

"You gotta marry the captain." Izzy grinned.

The other boys hooted and hollered and young Eugene grew red as a beat, "Not on your life!" said he, looking pleased.

Izzy frowned, shook her sword, and hollered at the top of her lungs "If it's to be a mutiny then so be it!" A fight ensued which ended in Lord Riley scolding Izzy, hiding his smile as he untied the ribbons that imprisoned Young Mr Dunsworth to a cherry tree. Isabel was running wild, her curls flying free.

Chapter 2

As they grew older the Riley Twins, as close to each other as ever sisters could be, showed such astounding differences in character that any who knew them declared if it weren't for their similar looks one could never assume they were siblings.

Both girls, in their early teen years, were of average height, both already had covetable curves despite being considered too thin, both had big grey eyes (that looked almost blue when they were wearing that particular colour, and so they often wore it) and blond hair (although it should be mentioned Isabel's was considered ashy-blond while Miranda's was considered golden).

Though they were pretty children, as they grew older no one would ever comment on them being great beauties. Miranda was considered the handsomer twin (though it was difficult to tell one from the other unless they were stood beside each other) and this was a good thing, for Isabel cared less for her looks than her sister and did not mourn over them as Miranda did (their figures were to awkwardly gangly, her nose too big, her eyes so bland – she hated the color gray). Despite what Miranda so bitterly thought of herself they had much growing yet to do and would age into their features elegantly.

Isabel continued to love the outdoors, walking, boating, fishing, drawing in the fields.

Miranda began to gravitate towards the shops with her friends, the library with romantic novels (though, admittedly, Isabel too could often be found engrossed in a suspenseful volume), loved parties – even though she wasn't yet old enough to join the adults and young ladies who had already been presented. Miranda dreamed of the day of her 'coming out'.

Isabel was spontaneous and wild in the presence of those she was closest with, and reserved among acquaintances and strangers; her conversation quick, thoughtful, and mature.

Miranda was playful and outgoing with everyone, everywhere; and though, when required, she could enjoy intelligent and genteel conversation, she preferred to talk about the latest fashions and members of the opposite sex.

On their fifteenth birthday they were thrown a large party and played Annie Over in the warmth of an early summer sun. Three girls watched from the sidelines with the older ladies, one of these was Miranda; she clapped and gleefully shouted support to her sister's team. Isabel's aim was superb; having caught the ball, she lobbed it expertly at the runner from the other team hitting him solidly on the shoulder. His team groaned as they lost another member to Isabel's.

"It is sinful for a girl to throw so well." the boy grinned good-naturedly, squeezing between she and young Dunsworth.

"It is sinful you dodge so ill." Dunsworth retaliated with a flash of irritation in his eyes for being pushed from his seat. Isabel smiled to herself.

"I'll get her back. I'll get you back Miss Riley, just wait you." The boy threatened teasingly.

The game ended. Isabel's team lost, she blamed it on Mr Westbrook, claiming he was now too old for the game; for now that he was a man he was too big a target and too slow. Mr Westbrook was offended. Miranda told Isabel not to be unkind. Matthew told them they were dirty hooligans. Miranda replied unkindly.

The day had begun to heat to the point where games were no longer fun, and the partiers retreated to shade. Miranda sat in the shadow of a cherry tree with the rest of the girls and boys while the staff cleaned up their game, and Isabel went walking with her cousin Charity Lawrence, followed at a short distance by eighteen-year-old Eugene Dunsworth and another older boy.

"How loyal those boys are in their pursuit of Miss Lawrence." One girl laughed.

"Nay," another boy returned "Dunsworth is not one to pursue. The young Duke no doubt requested Dunsworth walk with him to save face. He has laid claim on fair Miss Lawrence and none of the rest of us men stand a chance against his charms." he finished begrudgingly.

Miranda laughed. "I'm sure he would seem less charming were he not quite so rich!"

"And Miss Lawrence would be less beautiful if her dowry were not so plump." a girl snickered, and was joined by the others. Miranda did not laugh.

"Oh, do not be so sour." her friends teased. "how bias you are!"

The girl who made the joke about Charity's plump dowry spoke again as the four subjects of their conversation disappeared down the path which led into a little wood. "We should follow them and play chaperone. We will no doubt catch them playing games for two." the group laughed and stood to sneak after the walkers.

Miranda did not think they would find anyone being the least bit flirtatious; nevertheless, she happily led the group along the Tenby trails.

~~~

"I don't quite like the idea of you having to move so far away from us." Isabel was lamenting to her cousin.

"London is not so very far away dearest."

"But if only Uncle could have chosen Bath, it is closer by miles!"

"Opportunity arises precisely where it wishes to, not where we wish it... Unfortunately. Papa had no choice."

"Ah, and you will be presented in London next year, not here at dear Tenby as we always planned! Now we cannot abscond with you afterwards and force you to tell us every detail! Miranda will be especially sorry about that."

Young Miss Charity laughed. "But you forget I can write you!"

"It is not the same!" Isabel grinned.

Hearing voices behind them, the cousins turned to glance at who was behind.

"Mr Dunsworth." Isabel commented in a low voice.

"And the young duke."

"Mr Bertram is not yet a duke. I wish people would not call him that."

"His father is old, and very ill, he will be soon."

"It is sinfully insensitive to anticipate another's death."
~~~

"How dramatic you are. Very well, now you have caused me guilt, I will refrain from attaching a title to him until it becomes appropriate."

They emerged from the woods into a small clearing that dropped very suddenly into an odd little valley with a creek running through. A branch of the trail led to a large gazebo at the edge of this drop, which overlooked the creek below where small game loved to rest and drink. Isabel and Miss Lawrence headed to this gazebo and sat to converse in the shade within.

The girls did not necessarily wish to be joined by anyone, for neither of them preferred an excess of company (an excess to them being a company of more than two or three); but it must be admitted that they had quite taken a fancy to the young gentlemen who followed them – Miss Lawrence having developed a recent affection for Mr Bertram and Miss Riley having harbored affections for Mr Dunsworth since the at least the age of eight – and so it followed, when said gentlemen approached with the request to join them, the two ladies allowed it happily.

Dunsworth knew his friend held a torch for young Miss Lawrence and took initiative in monopolizing Miss Riley's attention (much to her barely concealed delight) in order for Bertram to capture the attention of the other.

The boys took pride in how smoothly their machinations played out; as though if the ladies had been any less willing it would have played out the same.

"Does your father not hunt them?" Dunsworth quietly asked Miss Riley, standing against the railing looking down at the deer sleeping below.

"No, not here. Papa wishes his game to have a sanctuary lest the creatures of Tenby are hunted to extinction."

"That is wise enough."

The two of them glanced towards Miss Lawrence and Bertram, who had already exited the gazebo and began down the walk together...alone. Dunsworth frowned.

"My cousin knows better than to go without a chaperone, they should not have gone." Isabel muttered.

"Yes, and by doing so they have left us alone, this is a disagreeable predicament." Dunsworth added in irritation.

"...shall we follow them?" she suggested regretfully.

"That would be wise." He straightened and turned just as she did. Her shoe hit his boot and she stumbled. Eugene Dunsworth caught her fall, the process of which ended in them tucked into an awkward hug; flustered, they quickly stepped apart.

"Oh Ho! What have we here!" a jovial male voice startled them. Both Dunsworth and Isabel flushed with embarrassment as the group of boys and girls Miranda Riley led began to laugh and tease.

Miranda attempted to support her sister. "Oh do hush you lot, I'm certain it is not as it seems!"

"It is not!" Isabel gasped out, "Miss Lawrence left with Mr Bertram and we were just about to follow and.." Dunsworth interrupted.

"She tripped. I was merely catching her fall."

"There see?" laughed Miranda.

"Oh a likely story!" another girl giggled, causing the group to burst forth in mirthful teasing once more. Dunsworth sighed with aggravation and left down the trail. Isabel stood silent in frustration and embarrassment. The group of youths dispersed down the trail, but Miranda tarried behind with her sister.

"I am sorry Izzy; they didn't mean any harm by it."

"I know..." Isabel sat dejectedly "I know but he seems so strong in his morals that I feel it would anger him to be so wrongfully accused. I'm sure he feels his reputation has been besmirched and his pride is injured and I am the cause of it. He will avoid me for the rest of eternity I am sure of it."

"Oh how dramatic you are sister!" Miranda laughed a little, then comforted. "He will not avoid you for eternity, that would be impolite; and he seems the stiffly proper type who would loath to be impolite."

Isabel did not look entirely comforted. She heaved a sigh, "I thought perhaps we could finally become friends, now it is ruined."

"Izzy love, you really must get over your infatuation with Mr Dunsworth; this is childish fancy, you will find someone much better suited for you I know."

"You only think him ill-suited because he will inherit only four-thousand pounds at most."

"I do not mean to sound material, but though his family may have the respectability to pass in our circles, they have not quite the wealth to be considered your equal. And more than that, I do not see how you can find him attractive; he is no taller than you, his hair is too long, and his face is so covered with blemishes he looks as though he's acquired the pox."

"That is very prejudiced of you; He can't help if his skin has an excess of pustules. You get them too sometimes. He is still very handsome despite them, and he will grow taller, and perhaps cut his hair in a more fetching style."

Miranda rolled her eyes. "If you say so. When we are older we will be able to choose whomever we wish – something many girls aren't at leisure to do – It would not be wise to save yourself for the Dunsworth boy and potentially miss out on a more agreeable match."

"A more agreeable match being one who is more rich I assume." Isabel commented sardonically.

Miranda laughed, then sighed dreamily. "Nay, one who is handsome and romantic, and cherishes you and treats you like a princess. Although, him being shockingly rich would be a bonus."

"You are incorrigible!" Isabel grinned "Come, let us find where Cousin Charity has run off to with Mr Bertram."

Cousin Charity Lawrence became Lady Bertram not eight months later.

Chapter 3

During their adolescent years the twins spent the great majority of the time developing their accomplishments.

They learned French, Spanish, Italian, and Latin (Miranda thought Latin unnecessary and boring until Isabel reminded her of their studies on ancient Rome; then Miranda thought it a language of luxury and romance and Isabel thought Miranda silly).They practiced piano until they were proficient in all the classics and could write pieces of their own.They sang beautifully, their voices maturing with age; Miranda's voice becoming rich and soft (and sultry by design, much to her sister's disgust), and Isabel's sweet and clear.They read as many books as they could get their hands on (Miranda still loving romances and mysteries and Isabel still preferring adventures and books of information), they decorated hats and arranged flowers and wrote letters with precise and flowing hand.Miranda wrote poems and ballads as often as she could, and Isabel wrote poems begrudgingly when instructed to by the governess.They acquired as much knowledge of politics and history as was necessary for a lady (Isabel acquiring more than was necessary, much to her governess's delight and her sister's chagrin) and were always up to date on the latest trends and fashions.They carried themselves and danced with such grace their dancing instructor considered them his best pupils; as though if they paid him less he would love them the same.

When asked by Lord Riley, Elizabeth Lawrence declared them most accomplished young ladies and most definitely ready to be presented this season, and if you asked her they had been ready to be presented last year. Lord Riley was reluctant, but agreed that since most girls were presented at sixteen or seventeen it was reasonable they be presented now, at eighteen.

He steeled himself, looking no longer at young men as boys but as wolves stalking their prey; any wolf to approach one of his little lambs would be doing so under the watchful eye of their protective father.

There was to be an elaborate summer house party at Tenby Hall for the girls' coming out into society; a week, beginning with a ball and ending with a ball five days following. Games and dinners and excursions were planned; every day must be eventful lest any of the one-hundred-fifty-or-more guests find themselves neglected or bored.

The girls were very put out when a note came from Westbrook stating his business in London, which had kept him away for nearly five weeks already, may hold him in Town until after their party; but their spirits were lifted again when Aunt Lawrence arrived two weeks in advance to help prepare; bringing with her fabulous gowns for the girls.

Miranda was beside herself with joy being fitted and draped for hours on end; Dinner dresses, ball gowns, walking dresses, riding habits. Isabel was less enthusiastic, exhausted after a day of standing in one place, anxious in anticipation of being stabbed by a pin (though it happened only once).

Lord and Lady Bertram were expected a week before the ball, but their carriage broke a wheel so they would not arrive until later. Cousin Edwin Lawrence arrived they day his sister was meant to.

The closer time drew to the party the more palpable the excited tension grew; the promise of long nights full of music, desserts, and dancing was forefront in the minds of the twins, and the men welcomed the opportunity to converse on topics of parliament.

Two days before the event the great hall was abuzz with the bustle of servants as last-minute preparations were made for the first ball of the season; the Tenby Hall staff were run off their feet readying rooms, entertainment, and delicacies to carry over the next seven days. After an evening of gleefully chasing butterflies and adding new grass-stains to their old 'walking' dresses, Isabel and Miranda Riley walked into the sitting room to see a new arrival stood chatting with their father and Cousin Edwin.

"Em! Izzy!" the girls' father smiled, waving his daughters in. "Come see who has also come early!" The twins immediately recognized the tall young man who turned to greet them, with unkempt mahogany hair threatening to obstruct mischievous grey eyes. His lazy smile did not charm them as it did other ladies (not that he realized this inherent charm).

"Matthew!" Isabel exclaimed joyfully, running to clutch one of his arms. "You have come!"

"You!" Miranda laughed as she grasped his other arm and scolded. "What misery we have endured thinking you would abandon us during such a pivotal point in our lives!"

"Ah but look, is not my presence now rightly appreciated?" He smirked playfully. "I had to leave you girls in suspense lest I be taken for granted."

Isabel scoffed and Miranda returned, "What pomp! Arrogance does not look well on you Matthew!"

The trio took a seat on the plush settee and Westbrook rested his arms on the back of it, a twin on either side. Lord Riley peered over the top of his paper at them as they bantered together on the couch. He folded it and took up his coffee from the side table, commenting casually before taking his sip, "You know what this house party represents I assume, Matthew."

"The girls announcing they are ready to leave the nest." Westbrook grinned.

"Yes, we are ladies now." Isabel smiled.

"So you must begin treating us likewise!" Miranda finished.

"You'd best behave Westbrook." Edwin Lawrence laughed.

Matthew snorted disagreeably. "The day I believe you two have become ladies is the day I'll eat my cravat! Especially this one," he looked to Miranda, squeezing an arm around her shoulder, then turned back to Izzy to inform, "There is dirt on her nose; I think she needs a few more years, she's not quite presentable material yet. My reputation couldn't risk being seen with her."

Miranda gasped at him in indignation as Isabel guffawed. She removed his arm from around her and dumped it unceremoniously in his lap, applying a handkerchief vigorously to the imaginary dirt spot. "Well then, Matthew, if you think you're such a catch do feel free to flirt with all the ladies at Saturday's Ball. I for one think you are a troll, and I'd willingly eat your cravat as well rather than burden you with my un-ladylike company!" Mr Westbrook's arm returned to her shoulders.

Lord Riley cleared his throat and spoke seriously. "They are considered young ladies now, being eighteen, and of marriageable age."

Mr Westbrook's face took on an expression of alarm, then shame, and he quickly placed his hands in his lap. Isabel and Miranda also settled down quickly, scooting to make more space between themselves and their male friend. They all sat in chagrined silence.

"Gracious Papa, how severe you are." Miranda muttered. Lord Riley continued reading his paper. Edwin Lawrence chuckled.

Chapter 4

<hr>

Before the twins went to sleep that night, they went through their new wardrobes, planning their outfits for the week. While Isabel began to feel her nerves at the thought of entering a ball for the first time with so many eyes on her, Miranda was exuberant! Her mind wandered to daydreams of romantic encounters, dancing by moonlit lakes with a true love, or being rescued from some terrible fate. She giggled at a particularly scandalous girlish fancy, twirling as she clutched a blue gown, making Isabel glance at her with a raised eyebrow.

"What are you dreaming of?"

"Ah nothing, just a daydream. You know, when I fall in love it will be with a true romantic, who is thoughtful, and will treasure me, and want to spoil me with gifts and compliments; not that I am so material that I expect gifts and compliments or think myself deserving of gifts and compliments, but it would be preferable that my partner in life think me deserving of such things. 'His reputation couldn't risk being seen with me'...really! I can't understand why he takes such delight in my distress!"

Isabel, holding a copper silk dinner dress to her frame, laughed outright. "Gracious, he wounded you deeply this evening!"

"He did not wound me!..." She handed the blue dress to her ladies maid to put away and pulled out a pink taffeta. "It is just frustrating that he still treats us like his little sisters. We are not little anymore, we are of age to be considered women and should be treated as such. He is so childish, he will never find a wife!"

"He only teases us because we are his family and he is comfortable with us. And do not be cruel, I'm sure he will find a wife someday."

"Yes, and I hope soon, it would be perfection to have a sister-friend living so nearby; and it would be good for him to have a woman's touch." Miranda discarded the pink taffeta and hopped onto their bed, waggling her eyebrows suggestively.

"Em!"

"In his house! And manners! Heavens Izzy, what were you thinking!" She chucked a pillow at her sister.

"I do agree with you though, about having a sister-friend in Thornhill." the elder tucked her knees under her chin. "It must be lonely for him, living there by himself all those years since his parents died."

"Yes." Miranda agreed thoughtfully, then smiled. "It is no wonder he has spent nearly every day with us since his parents passed." They crawled under the blankets and snuggled there as they spoke. "Ooh Izzy! We should find him a match! What fun that would be!"

"Yes! I think we know him well enough to choose him a suitable wife, then we are certain to like whomever he marries! I think this will work, as long as you cease matchmaking for yourself long enough to matchmake for him!"

"Oh hush you, I am not so desperate for a match as you seem to think I am!" Ignoring her sister's cry of 'you are!' she continued overtop her. "Oh I cannot wait for tomorrow night!" Miranda let out a rapturous sigh.

"I can! I am sick thinking of it!"

~~~

They rose early the following morning, discontent to tarry in bed when anticipation kept them from slumber. At the unholy hour of nine they were bathed and perfumed and finishing dressing themselves. Isabel tucked some lace behind the square neckline of her day dress as Miranda's ladies maid prettied her hair and smoothed her pleated pale-blue skirts.

The day seemed to fly by with the flurry of last minute set-up. Draperies were being hung on balconies and pillars, flowers were brought in to decorate the entry hall where there would be refreshments and places to sit, massive bouquets adorned the grand ballroom and banquet hall. Guests had been arriving all day and rooms and meals were ready for them. Aunt Lawrence was busy instructing staff, Isabel and Miranda helping her to test pastries and check and re-check lists until the clock struck one-o'clock. The twins had a casual one-o'clock lunch together in their room; Isabel finished first and left to find Aunt, and Miranda stayed to watch the maid's progress on ironing their presentation gowns.

looking out a window Miranda spotted a carriage she thought she recognized and, hoping cousin Charity Bertram had finally arrived from London, jumped up to rush and greet her. In her haste to descend the stairs she nearly bowled Westbrook over on his ascent.

"Watch yourself clumsy." he grinned good naturedly

"Hush! Oh, Matthew," she halted him on the stairs. "have you heard who it is who comes up the drive just now??"

"No one handsome or wealthy so you won't want to bother going down."

"Oh you would imply I'm so shallow!"
~~~

"Are you not?" said with a raised eyebrow and a sly smile.

"Ouf!" Miranda huffed and turned to ignore him, continuing on her path to the entry hall.

Once outside she saw her favorite cousin already animatedly speaking to her mother and Isabel and ran to embrace her. After greeting Cousin Charity and Bertram warmly, Miranda was introduced to a cousin of Bertram's who had travelled with them.

Grace Cotton was to turn eighteen in two months' time and was in her second season. She was a petite little thing with thick nearly-white-blond hair falling tastefully out of it's bun. Her wide blue eyes and un-naturally pink, full lips made her look like a doll, and her gentle way of talking and carrying herself was so endearing to the twins they fell immediately in love with her.

The ball would begin in a very few hours so everyone dispersed to their rooms to ready themselves for the grand, formal affair.

~~~

Isabel and Miranda grasped their bedposts firmly as their abigails reefed on the cords of their corsets. Letting out their breaths once they were tied off they stepped into their voluminous white ball gowns. They were identical in style; delicate strings of glittering diamond-like crystals dripped from the slim band around their necks to where they were attached on the low bodice of the silk empire-waist gowns. Short sleeves drooped off the shoulders and the skirts pooled into a long train that their abigails were just now fastening to the white silk bracelets they wore on their wrists. Not wanting to be mistaken one for the other, the Grecian inspired trim decorating the sleeves, bodice, and hem were different colors: Isabel's silver, and Miranda's pale gold.
~~~

While they dressed and had their hair done Miranda chattered on in nervous excitement, while the knots in Isabel's stomach (growing more tight and sickening as Miranda spoke) kept her mostly silent.

"Mercy, there are so many people! I shall not know who to approach first! I have already seen a good sixty or more this afternoon, the greater majority of whom we have never met before I am sure, and lawd knows we will see most arriving just on time for the first dance to begin, or fashionably late. It looks to me as though Aunt has failed to invite enough ladies, there will be some men without partners every dance! Not that men would be so affected by that as ladies, no doubt they prefer sitting some dances out; but maybe not, I suppose it is a matter of character and some men are more lively than others, just as it is with ladies. It is actually vexing, Izzy, we have not yet seen any young men so far whom we would consider really attractive. Many seem passable enough I suppose, but I suppose a truly handsome man is a rare thing to come by don't you agree?"

Isabel concurred weakly.

"Oh! I am keeping an eye out for a lady for our Mr Westbrook. I think it would be a splendid thing if he were to fall in love with dear Miss Cotton, what think you?!"

"I think she is too reserved for him, I think he would prefer someone a little more animated."

"I believe you are wrong. He teases us relentlessly for being unladylike despite my unceasing efforts to prove him wrong. He calls us loud, and improper...and shallow. If that doesn't speak of him as a man who prefers genteel ladies I don't know what does."

"Nay Em, you judge his character badly. He is playful, he says those things because he knows they will irk us. You know how he chases you with frogs and snakes – I haven't the slightest idea why you run from him by the way, as we used to catch them as pets and you liked them well enough then – and he is wild when we play games with him outdoors. He would be bored with a quiet, proper wife, I'm sure of it."

"I agree his is playful; he is very much a kindred spirit to us, therefore, if we find Miss Cotton endearing and lovable, would he not then also?"

"Very well, we can introduce them but I believe we should let things develop naturally between them; if anything is to develop. I am still unconvinced."

"It is settled." Miranda smiled contentedly, turning before the mirror as her ladies maid threaded a string of diamonds through her intricate psych knot. She pulled at the curls that framed her face. "Enough of this talk, it must be nearly time for us to go down now."

Isabel's stomach clenched. "Aunt.."

"Said she would come for us before the first dance, I know. Is your first dance with Matthew or did you claim Papa?"

"Papa." Isabel muttered.

"Oh very well. I suppose I am promised to the former than." Miranda snatched up her empty dance card and fastened it to her bracelet with her train. "Don't forget yours."

Isabel picked up her dance card reluctantly as Miranda paced. A knock on the door and Aunt entered.

"Oh hurrah!" Miranda cried.

Isabel felt as though she might cast up her accounts.

Chapter 5

Standing by the drinks table in the Hall, Matthew Westbrook was discussing estate matters with Edwin Lawrence when they heard Isabelle and Miranda being announced.

"Ah, the stars of the evening are arrived." Grinned Edwin. "It feels odd they are coming out already."

"It does feel as though they are still too young," Matthew chuckled "But they are now eighteen after all, and many girls have their first season at sixteen or seventeen."

"Yes, and many married at their age besides. Lawd!" Edwin laughed "My uncle was loath to put them out into society, I pity the men who set sail for them."

"I pity them as well, but less for fear of the father as the twins themselves. Isabel is a good enough girl, though quite a spitfire upon closer acquaintance. Em, however; it will take a special sort of man to satisfy her vanity." He laughed. "I try to keep it in check but she is not fond of being teased."

"How unexpected." Edwin responded sarcastically with a chuckle. The two men were walking towards the staircase where the twins had been announced.

"Ah I see Miss Cotton and my sister." observed Lawrence "She has the twins with her already. Look at those girls, they're proper ladies now, one couldn't rightly call them scrawny anymore. Good luck keeping Cousin Miranda's vanity in check now Matt, it seems she's attracting every bachelor in the country...but who is the shocking beauty of a girl with them, and the redhead?"

Matthew barely heard half of what Edwin spoke once he noticed the glittering figure in white and gold speaking with Charity Bertram. Miranda's pale yellow curls shone and glittered in the light of the chandelier and her beautifully long neck was adorned with an elegant choker streaming with diamonds. Miranda turned to greet them with a stunning smile and once her deep, grey eyes met his, everyone else in the ballroom faded away. His eyes lowered to her lips as she spoke, mesmerized by the look of them – so soft and full – until she turned to Charity again and he felt a subtle smack on his arm.

"Ay Matt, wake up man," Edwin gave him an odd look "we're getting the ladies drinks. Have you had one to many already?"

"I have not!" Matthew defended, following Edwin.

"Good lord my man, you couldn't keep your eyes off her and never spoke a word! Are you usually this subtle in your conquests??"

"What conquest!? Don't be ridiculous, I was merely thinking your mother best fire her seamstress, the bodice on the twins' dresses are shockingly low. Who was the redhead, and the other blond?" Matthew inquired. He frowned, realizing he did not recall introductions or the conversation just now, and felt ashamed at his rude behavior.

"Grace Cotton, the pretty little blond, is a cousin of my brother-in-law, Bertram." Lawrence was explaining. "The tittering ginger hyena is Victoria Bradshaw, a new friend of theirs; one of the Bradshaws from Bristol recently moved to London."

"Ah right, her father is a judge is he not"

"That's the one. She simpered quite forcefully at you when Em said you were too rich for your britches or something of the sort."

"Thanks for the warning." Matthew grinned, then, "Em said what??"

~~~

The girls, Meanwhile, were taking advantage of the men's absence in order to gossip. Victoria started with a giggle "That Mr Westbrook is shamefully attractive, how do you girls not see it! It is true then, that he has nearly twenty thousand a year?!"

Miranda wrinkled her nose "Nearly indeed." she scoffed "He is a good six thousand pounds short. In any case, character trumps looks and riches and he is an awful nuisance!"

"Oh Em, he is not so bad, I know you do not believe that! Miranda is still sore from him calling her shallow the other day." Isabel defended. "He is a brother to us, we could never see him in any other way."

"He didn't seem a nuisance," Miss Cotton said gently "In fact it seemed he was quite taken with you Miranda."

"Heavens no!" Miranda laughed "I will echo my sister; he is our brother. I guarantee he was trying to find something to tease me about!"

"Ah, look, someone approaches." Mrs Bertram announced quietly "Surely he won't be so bold as to speak without an introduction..."
~~~

Seeing the tall blond young man stride toward them Miranda determined him the only truly attractive man in the room and hoped he would be so bold. He gave a little bow and spoke.

"Miss Cotton," said he with a voice so caressingly smooth it could coax honey from a bear.

"Would you do me the honor of introducing me to your friends?"

"You know this gentleman?" Inquired Isabel.

"Yes, we have met before." Miss Cotton replied a little tightly. "Mr Kirkley, meet Miss Miranda Riley, Miss Isabel Riley, Mrs Charity Bertram, and Miss Victoria Bradshaw. Ladies, Mr William Kirkley."

He acknowledged each lady in turn. "A great pleasure to make your acquaintance. I have heard much of the Riley twins, I am surprised no one mentioned how classically beautiful you two are, I find myself unprepared."

Isabel and Miranda smiled their thanks for the compliment, brushing it off. Isabel thought him ridiculous. Miranda thought him charming. Miss Bradshaw raised an eyebrow and looked away.

"I hope it is not too bold of me to request a dance from all of you ladies;" He turned to Miranda, capturing her with his blue eyes and wide charming smile, she felt her heart begin to race. "and I especially hope there are a few blank spaces left on your dance card Miss Riley?"

She gave him a brilliant smile. "By all means Mr Kirkley," then with a laugh "I'm sure we could make a space even if there weren't."

"Miranda.." Isabel frowned.

"Oh you are insensitive to your opposing sex." Mr Kirkley jested with Miranda. "You can say I bullied you for it and I shall take the blame."

"My hero," she smiled, fluttering her lashes "but that is unnecessary, you see? There are still quite a few dances left unclaimed." Miranda extended the wrist from which her dance card hung to him.

Kirkley's fingers brushed her wrist as he took up her card, giving her tingles even through the fabric of their gloves. He turned away with a subtle wink. She took up her card to see he had written his name in at least four spaces, including the first dance!

Mr Westbrook and Mr Lawrence then returned with their drinks and the ladies introduced them to Mr Kirkley. The first chords of the first dance began and Mr Westbrook held his hand out to Miranda.

"Ooh, Ma..Mr Westbrook. I'm so sorry, I forgot you had my first dance and now I have promised it to Mr Kirkley! Would you be terribly put out if I.."

"No not at all," Mr Westbrook relented, looking terribly put out. "You will make it up to me during the course of the night I assume?"

"Of course!" She smiled, not noticing his irritation, and wrote his name on her card before stepping onto the floor with Mr Kirkley. He was a wonderful dancer she thought (not that she had any to compare him to) and she thoroughly enjoyed their flirtatious banter, giggling and blushing the dance away; at the end of it she found her sister and brandished her card for Isabel to see.

"Oh, dear, that is fodder for gossip. You cannot stand up with him that often at your first ball, with so few ladies in attendance. I must say, Em love, I am a little disappointed you used Matthew so ill; it was unkind of you to brush him aside so, it is not right to break promises and you did promise him the dance; he was forced to sit it out. It would have been more appropriate for have your first dance in your first season with a man you are familiar with – like a father or brother."

"Don't start acting so uppity and proper Izzy, you would have done the same had Mr Dunsworth asked for your first."

"I would not!"

"You would! Ha! I knew you still held a torch for him. I had hoped you would have been over that by now."

"I just wish to make it through our first season without scandal." Isabel explained, ignoring her sister's comment. They were interrupted by Miss Bradshaw.

"La, I am jealous," the girl pouted her thin lips as she joined them. "Mr Kirkley is a dream, and his family is nearly as wealthy as yours!"

"I would not go so far as to consider him a dream." Miss Cotton said thoughtfully, joining them

"As Miss Miranda Riley said earlier, a man is more than wealth and stature."

Victoria interjected with a snicker. "I saw you looking at him too, I bet you're more jealous than I am!" The girls giggled.

Miss Cotton did not respond to the girl's teasing and Miranda, noticing her discomfort, changed the subject, "Is there anyone else here from Bristol, Miss Bradshaw, do you know?" Miss Cotton smiled at her in thanks.

"There are one or two other families I here I recognize from there; one family has an oldest son who has barely tolerable looks but there is no one else worth knowing in Bristol; I'm glad we are moved to London." Miss Bradshaw sneered up her nose, then with a gasp she stared at the entry to the ballroom and pointed her fan, with a shocking lack of subtlety, in that general direction. "Oh Oh! But who is that!" and the three other girls turned as inconspicuously as possible to see who Miss Bradshaw was in raptures over now. There was no question who the object of their gaze was meant to be for the eyes of every lady in the room were captured the moment they laid eyes on him.

"I do not know him.." Miss Cotton started as the twins spoke overtop her.

"Isabel, that couldn't possibly be.." Isabel finished her sister's sentence "Eugene Dunsworth."

"I have not heard of him. Where does he reside? How much is he worth?" Miss Bradshaw pried.

"Only about three or four thousand a year." Miranda replied, as Isabel informed "His family resides in Southamptons."

"With a face like that I would be more than willing to overlook a small fortune, and four thousand is not at all small." Miss Bradshaw giggled, fluttering her fan before her face coquettishly. Her eyes squinted. "Who is that woman with him?"

"His sister I believe." offered Isabel after a glance at the graceful beauty in beige beside Dunsworth. Her raven hair was cut in a boyishly short style few women dared sport and encircled with a Grecian band. Isabel did not hear what the other girls said in response for her eyes had met with those of Eugene Dunsworth's and her heart was in her throat. While Miranda commented how he had grown taller and how stylish the cut of his hair and wondered at how clear his skin now was and gushed with the others over how gorgeous a male specimen he had turned out, Isabel was drowned by feelings she thought had faded over time, but in fact had only matured. She stepped forward to approach and greet him, as would have been entirely appropriate what with the ball being in her own home and they not being entirely unknown to each other, but at the memory of their last encounter – being caught in an awkward situation that questioned their good reputation, he agitated and she mortified – she found she could not approach him; and then her opportunity was gone as another, older, lady greeted him and his sister, stealing his attention.

The course of the evening insisted on passing far too quickly. Isabel Riley was desperate to speak to Young Mr Dunsworth and, more so, dance with him; but something within her insisted she avoid him. Perhaps it was the deep-rooted and misplaced belief that he resented her for the teasing he endured that day so long ago; perhaps she merely knew not what to say once she was before him and her overabundance of thought on the subject caused her too much anxiety to follow through.

The last dance before dinner she felt fingers brush her shoulder and turned to see the object of her violent affections suddenly before her. She felt ill and, in contrast, also euphorically happy. Mr Dunsworth asked her to dance and she accepted shakily. He complimented the decor and general ambiance politely before commenting eventually that it had been some time since they saw each other last.

"Yes. Just over three years by a month." she confirmed, then added quickly with a flush. "I believe! I believe it's been...about that." she shut her mouth with a cringe.

After a few chords, "Are you enjoying your first ball then?"

"I am. Though I find it is exhausting, so many people and so much dancing. Not that I'm not enjoying it!...the dancing I mean...and the people are lovely, I do appreciate their coming of..of course!" She stuttered, distressed he may think she was not enjoying their dance, or didn't enjoy his company. He smiled a little. She struggled to find something more to say. Did he wish her to speak? Or did he enjoy dancing without conversation once in a while? Isabel herself quite enjoyed a silent dance without the obligation of entertaining one's partner with comments on the number of dancers or recent weather; but perhaps that was odd. Isabel felt as though she ought to say something lest he find her awkward or boring, but she could not think of anything, and with her mind all apanic and not at all focused on the dance, her feet forgot a step causing her to stumble.

Dunsworth's brows rose as he helped her back into step so quickly and smoothly that no one noticed the misstep but he and she. Isabel was now in the depths of despair and she forced tears of mortification not to show in her eyes.

The dance ended and Dunsworth led her to the side and with a small bow and a polite smile "Thank you for the dance Miss Riley, it was an honor and great pleasure." to which she could only nod and return his smile for fear of her voice shaking if she spoke.

He turned to exit towards the dining hall, and with him finally gone Isabel took herself to an inconspicuous corner to groan loudly and depressedly into her gloved hands and take a few deep calming breaths before joining the others for dinner.

Chapter 6

To Miranda Riley's dismay, she was joined by Matthew Westbrook for the meal. A little uncomfortably sheepish after her conversation with Isabel earlier, she sat between him and Cousin Charity Bertram and her eyes searched to see where Mr Kirkley was seated. She finally met his eyes a ways down the table.

Matthew, sitting between Miranda and Miss Cotton, had noted the actions and conversation between his honorary sister and the object of her interest (being Mr Kirkley), and had grown increasingly irritated as the night carried on, especially as each dance passed without Miranda giving him his promised one. Seeing Miranda and William Kirkley now exchanging titillated looks and smiles over the cold cuts and baked veggies his irritation peeked. He leaned so only she could hear. "Do you really find that silly fop attractive?" He tried to tease, but in truth it almost came out as a sneer.

She glared at him "He is not silly, he is a playful romantic. And just because he takes extra care in his appearance doesn't make him a fop. You could learn a little of romance and wooing a woman, than you may find love and not find yourself alone the rest of your life."

Matthew wasn't overly successful on hiding how that comment pricked him. "That's all very nice but romance has precious little to do with love. Your gentleman can't keep you alive and happy on flattery alone."

Miranda ignored his comment and took some sweetmeats from the plate a Butler proffered to her. Matthew let out a sharp sigh of frustration and struck up a conversation with Miss Cotton over the remainder of the meal who pleasantly surprised him with her knowledge and intelligent conversation. He learned at one point that she knew Mr Kirkley, they being both from London. Her manner when speaking of him didn't seem complimentary, but she no reason as to why she did not like the man; not that Matthew cared enough about gossip to pry.

~~~

Isabel's luck was proving ill, she found herself a seat and who but Miss Dunsworth took the seat opposite and waved over her brother who had been chatting by the door. He sat with a nod to Isabel and her father (who sat next to her). Isabel ducked her head to hide her fierce blush, taking longer than necessary to fix her napkin in her lap.

Mr Riley struck up a conversation with Dunsworth immediately, asking how things were in Southamptons; Isabel eavesdropped for a very short time until she heard a bright feminine voice speaking her name. "I don't believe we have officially met, Miss Riley, the last time I saw you was on you and your sister's fifteenth birthday. I am Sicily Dunsworth, if you do not recall."

Isabel offered a tentative smile, "I remember you well though we only conversed in greeting, I have often regretted there was so little time for us to form a closer acquaintance." (Miss Dunsworth looked pleased) "It doesn't feel so long ago, but a suppose it has been quite some years."

"No, indeed, time does seem to speed by.." There was a pause.
~~~

"Will you be in London at all this season?"

"Not this year. We are to go to Bath for three weeks after this, then home to Southamptons."

"Oh I do love Bath!" Isabel cried, forgetting her nerves in her enthusiasm. "I have fond memories of our Aunt taking us bathing there in our youth and long to go again."

"Oh, you love the baths, how splendid! I also love bathing but we have never been to Bath before and have no acquaintance there, nor any idea of the best spots to go. You wouldn't happen to be going would you?"

"I wish I were, but nay! We have no plans yet to go anywhere for the rest of the season; but that may change, I will hope for bath. But you are lucky to live so close to the sea, for you may go sea-bathing whenever you wish."

"Not quite whenever I wish," Miss Dunsworth laughed "There are few good beaches and even fewer good days! I would not go sea-bathing unless the weather proved exceptionally hot (for the sea is quite chilly) and that is a difficult thing to predict; there are no beaches close enough to hop off to at a whim on a hot day."

"Oh how unfortunate! Do you have a lake at home then?"

"No," Miss Dunsworth sighed "Our estate does not have all the luxuries of yours. We only have a little pond and there are many trout in it, so if I wish to bathe in it I must be prepared to smell like a fish for a good two days after."

Isabel laughed, then leaned in to say conspiratively "Well as you are here for the week, we shall have to try and sneak a dip in one of our lakes! What say you to that?"

"I say yes!" Miss Dunsworth grinned.

~~~

After dinner, dancing resumed, and Miranda Riley checked her card to see who she was to dance with next. Her mood soured at seeing Matthew Westbrook's name written in her writing. "Ah yes, the promised dance. I would enjoy the prospect more if he was at least trying to be agreeable this evening." She muttered irritably, and looked up to see the man himself strolling towards her.

"May I have the next dance?" Asked he, reaching out a hand and bowing slightly.

"I have little choice but to accept." She grumbled, taking his hand and being lead to the floor. As the music rolled over the room, she was surprised to find he was the best dance partner she'd had so far; not that she'd tell him.

"I see you've made good friends with Miss Cotton." She commented, glancing at him slyly to see his reaction.

"Yes, she's refreshingly mature in her conversation," he obliged – disappointing Miranda with the lack of affection in his voice towards the lady – "she doesn't flirt and gossip like most other ladies." He gave Miranda a pointed look.

She sighed. "Perhaps if you attempted a conversation with me, instead of using every opportunity to tease and treat me like a child, your opinion of me would be different."

Mr Westbrook considered this. "That is a fair point." he grinned, "Let us try a conversation."

"I know not what to say to you." Miranda laughed after a pause.

"How is your first ball?" He prompted, "Is it everything you imagined?"
~~~

"It is not quite so magical, I suppose, as what I imagined in my youth watching from the balustrade...but I am having quite possibly the best night of my life."

"Ah. Enjoying being the center of attention as usual."

"You promised you would not tease."

"You are right, I beg your forgiveness and will begin again...enjoying meeting new people and dancing the night away looking pretty and grown up?"

"Why Matthew, you think me pretty, and grown up??" she grinned.

"Hypocrite." He grinned back. "Now who teases?""

A few turns passed and she worked up courage to speak something that had been weighing on her. "I feel I must apologize."

"Whatever for?"

"You were promised the first dance with me and I dismissed you too easily. I must admit, Isabel did admonish me a little for standing up in my first dance with a stranger, and I suppose I could have been less rash; but that matters less to me than the thought that I may have offended you. I did not intend to, you know how I love you."

"I suppose, now you've said it." He replied, a funny feeling in his chest.

"And you forgive me?"

"I suppose I could, if you do me a favor."

"What will you have me do?" She asked skeptically.

"I shall think on it and call in the favor at some later date."

"Oh very well." she huffed. "You will no doubt forget about it so that works well for me." Westbrook merely smiled, determined not to forget that he might torment her with it in the near future.

~~~

Though Isabel's night had not started well in her opinion, after dinner it began to improve. She spent a dance or two on the sidelines conversing with Miss Dunsworth and watching people.

"That man your sister dances with, how is he related to you?"

"Oh he is not a relation in truth, we call him our brother, we have been close family friends for...our entire lives."

"Ah, and the gentleman my brother speaks with now? Is he not a relation?"

"Yes, Edwin Lawrence is our cousin; his sister, cousin Charity, is here as well, I should like to introduce you."

"How many families live near you, with girls your age?"

Isabel replied, a little taken aback by the abrupt subject change. "Oh none close enough for us to grow up with any bosom friends. Why do you ask?"

"Curiosity. I feel we could be great friends if it were not for the distance."

"The distance between Tenby Hall and Southamptons? I do not think it so very great. I could come visit you easily enough now that I am of age to travel alone...well, not entirely alo.."

Isabel was spoken over by Miss Dunsworth, "Would you? I should be very glad if you did."

Before Isabel could respond the current dance ended and a prettily plump middle-aged woman with raven hair approached, followed by a thin young man with a hooked nose who sported a thick stallion tail.
~~~

"Dear, I have someone who wished to be introduced to you, but before that," she smiled brightly, "I'd like to introduce myself to the young lady I see you becoming so chummy with. I am sure you have no memory of who I am Miss Riley."

"You are familiar; if I am correct you are Mrs Dunsworth, my companion's mother?"

"I am! And which twin am I speaking to? I can never tell you apart!"

"Isabel Mad'm." Isabel curtseyed a little with a smile. She caught Miranda's eye a little way away and was waved over. "I will leave you to your introductions, it appears my sister is summoning me. Miss Dunsworth, I am so glad to have made friends with you this evening."

"As am I." Miss Dunsworth smiled. Isabel departed. The hook-nosed man stared at her quite obviously as she left and she gave a polite smile, feeling slightly uneasy.

"What is it then?" She asked her sister upon reaching her and Miss Bradshaw.

"You have spent much time with Miss Dunsworth this evening, pray what do you think of her? Miss Bradshaw has overheard some shocking things."

"You should not gossip. I find her very pleasant; we have common interests and she is quite mature; as she should be, I assume she is nearly three-and-twenty."

"And not yet married, she will be an old maid." Miss Bradshaw snickered "But listen to this, many who know her family have mentioned she is quite odd, and I am inclined to agree, for their opinion of Miss Dunsworth derives from the lady's habit of swimming and sunbathing naked when alone at home!"

"Firstly," began Isabel, irritated. "how is this thing known if she does it when alone, and secondly, what business is it of anyone's what the lady does in the privacy of her own home."

"Gracious how defensive you are. You have to admit it is a bit irregular." Miranda put in.

"Yes, how defensive." Miss Bradshaw giggled. "You need not be, we all know you are only friends with the lady in order to gain the notice of the brother!"

"Miss Bradshaw that is wholly untrue!" Isabel gasped.

"Oh very well, I suppose you are wiser than to pursue a man of so lesser fortune than yourself, what a pity, for what a face. You will have to leave him for Miss Cotton or I." Miss Bradshaw lamented insincerely, and a movement behind her caught Isabel's eye. Three men had been standing and talking behind Miss Bradshaw, and the one directly behind her looked behind at the three girls as the lady spoke; Eugene Dunsworth's eyes met with Isabel's briefly before he looked away, appeared to excuse himself, and walked off. She felt every last drop of blood drain from her face.

"Izzy? Are you well?" Miranda asked.

"You must be more careful of what you say Miss Bradshaw! You are far too liberal with your opinions!" Isabel's dismay that Mr Dunsworth would now think badly of her was rapidly turning to fury towards Miss Bradshaw, she forced herself to stay kind and composed. "I..I think I must sit."

The other two girls, bewildered, led her to a nearby chaise. "Did I say something??" begged Miss Bradshaw. "I cannot think of anything I may have said to offend you."

"Miss Riley, may I have the next dance." A most feminine male voice interrupted. The three girls looked to the man who spoke, it was the hook-nosed young man who had only just introduced himself to Miss Dunsworth, and he was now speaking to Isabel. With a crease of confusion in her brow she looked to the ladies she had left barely a few minutes before and saw them watching her; Mrs Dunsworth looked mildly irritated while her daughter merely shrugged.

Isabel considered the night to have reached it's lowest point; things had begun to improve after her misstep dancing with Mr Dunsworth, but in the space of a few minute he had overheard a conversation that made her seem a coin-chaser and his mother and sister, it appeared, had now been shunned in favor of her company.

"Were you not just introduced to Miss Dunsworth by your own request, Sir? I'm certain she was your next dance partner?" She said as politely as possible.

"I considered it my lady, but who would continue to pursue a thistle when a rose presents itself." He said loudly with a smile that showed he thought himself irresistible.

"I am sorry I must decline sir; not just for the sake of my friend, but we have not yet been introduced; it would not be proper."

He straightened, his smile fading. He stood there a moment looking at her, then smiled again and, with a bow, departed.

"How shockingly forward." Miranda commented "Who was he? I did not like his manner."

Isabel opened her mouth to respond when they were interrupted again; Miss Bradshaw was asked to dance, followed by Mr Kirkley begging for Miranda to accompany him for the set. Isabel sat alone in her melancholy. As the clock chimed three and dawn threatened to appear, the partygoers one by one made their way to carriages or bedchambers and the Riley twins made their way to their own rooms.

Exhausted, Isabel thoroughly discontent and Miranda happily the opposite, they climbed out of their dresses and crawled into bed.

Chapter 7

The following afternoon brought on a myriad of activities to entertain the guests of Tenby hall. Most guests had gone home, but those who lived the greatest distances away stayed the week; thus, fifty-eight guests remained. Among them of note were Mr and Mrs Bradshaw and their daughter Miss Victoria Bradshaw, Mr and Mrs Dunsworth with their son and daughter, Mr Kirkley, the Mr and Mrs Lawrence, Mr Edwin Lawrence, Mr and Mrs Bertram and Miss Cotton who had come with them, and Mr Westbrook who lived near enough he was there every day in any case – these are all that pertain to our story. It was another unnaturally warm and sunny day, coaxing everyone outside to play croquet, walk the trails around Tenby's large lakes, and picnic on the estate lawns.

After a two o'clock tea outdoors, a group gathered for word games under the shade of the willows by the lake. Miss Bradshaw invited the Miss Rileys and Miss Dunsworth to play, who in turn invited Mr Westbrook – a persistent abundance of pleading and creative persuasion was required to gain his participation. Miranda convinced him in the end by reasoning that she also disliked word-games for they made little sense to her, yet she was obliging her friends and therefore could he not do the same for her sake? He agreed to join them if they convinced both Eugene Dunsworth and Edwin Lawrence to play as well. The girls' determination and skillfully applied charismatic charm brought them success.

Someone suggested they begin with 'connections', in which one would say three words and the others guessed what made them similar. Matthew, being forced to play first, offered 'knights', 'love', and 'hounds' to which Isabel correctly guessed 'loyalty'. Isabel followed with 'silk', 'chocolate', and 'tiger', the theme 'exotic' guessed correctly by her sister, making it Miranda's turn. A few turns passed and Mr Kirkley won a round. "I have prepared an easy one," declared he "calla lily, swan..." He paused for effect with a meaningful smile directed at Miranda Riley "Miss Riley."

"What?" Westbrook attempted to hold back a look of contempt with little success.

"Which Miss Riley? Do you not mean both of them?" Edwin Lawrence questioned.

"Miss Miranda Riley." Mr Kirkley verified, his gaze still on her and she encouraged him by returning his gaze with a coy look from beneath heavy lashes. Isabel and Matthew looked at each other with paralleled expressions of distaste.

"I believe the answer is meant to be either beauty or grace.." Miss Bradshaw nearly sneered.

"It is beauty, but grace also applies." Mr Kirkley confirmed, pleased to see Miranda's faint blush of pleasure as she bit her lip to hide a grin.

Charity Bertram furrowed her brow in confusion muttering to herself "I do not see how it makes sense to single out one sister in this instance, when they are so strikingly similar."

There was an uncomfortable silence which Miranda and Mr Kirkley seemed unaware of.

"This is a silly game." huffed Miss Bradshaw. "I am going to circle the lake, who will join me?" No one rose in response. With a stony face she stalked off alone. Mr Westbrook then stood, as did Dunsworth and Mr Lawrence, and the three men strode off together, relieved in their escape.

"As everyone is now leaving, why do we not go for a walk ourselves Miss Miranda? Miss Isabel, Mrs Bertram, won't you join us?" Mr Kirkley suggested amiably.

"Oh..I um..would love to but I see Miss Cotton just now and remembered something I wish to speak to her about. Do enjoy your walk you three." She hurried to greet Miss Cotton after a quick smile of apology for her cousin, who looked irritated at the prospect of playing lonely chaperone.

Under a refreshment tent, Isabel and Miss Cotton sat with Westbrook. They spoke at length about London and it's history. At one point Edwin Lawrence joined them, taking a seat on one of the lawn chairs between Matthew and Miss Cotton (who smiled beautifully in greeting) only to shortly after be summoned by a group of men to help solve a debate. Matthew was amused to see a subtle look of annoyance flash across his friends face at being made to abandon his place beside Miss Cotton to join them. During a pause in the conversation Isabel declared "It is a shame to let such a day waste by hiding from it, let us join those who are walking, the cool air off the lake will surely do us good." Her companions agreed and they took to the trails.

~~~

Miranda Riley and William Kirkley strolled closely together on one of Tenby's more thickly forested trails, with Mrs Bertram and her husband (whom she had recruited to walk with her) a few yards behind acting chaperone.
~~~

"I cannot stand an overly demure woman" Said Kirkley when asked his opinion on Miss Cotton "I infinitely prefer someone who can provide stimulating conversation and who shares my love for adventure!" He bent toward her as he walked "It is why I prefer your company vastly more than other ladies." He confessed.

She playfully smacked his arm with her fan "You make me blush Mr Kirkley! But I will return your compliment. You are far more agreeable a man than any I could name! Poor Miss Cotton, she has a sweet temper and I do like her; but you are right." Miranda giggled. "Although, there isn't much opportunity for adventure when chaperoned" She said with a pout.

They turned a corner in the twisting path and Mr Kirkley glanced behind to see the trees and foliage putting them momentarily out of sight of Mr and Mrs Bertram. He grabbed her hands suddenly with a playful twinkle in his eyes

"Let us lose them!" he whispered laughingly "Run!"

Miranda stifled her own giddy laugher as he pulled her along down the winding trail. She lifted her skirts to run more easily, looking behind in nervous excitement. Kirkley turned off the path suddenly, taking them into the forest, following a large slow stream leading away from the lake. "Mr Kirkley!" She gasped "We cannot, we may get lost!"

He stopped when they were out of sight of the path and drew her close, placing a finger on her lips with a sultry smile, and making her already racing heart skip. "Hush, we can follow the river back. Don't speak too loud or someone will hear us and our fun will be spoiled."

How bold he was, how dashing! Miranda was bewitched by the moment; an entranced, beloved heroine in a heart-pounding romance novel, more than willing – absolutely thrilled – to play the part. Chest rising and falling with rapid breath she gazed into his glittering blue eyes. Encouraged by the look she found there, and by the hands gently resting on her arms, she put her own hands on his chest and stepped into his embrace. He pushed an unruly golden strand off her face looking deep into her eyes. His fingers drew a path along her jaw to her chin, and tipped her face up towards his.

"Is it not too soon for this? I've known you but a day." She asked, her nerves finally beginning to send faint warning bells a-clanging in her brain.

He brushed his thumb gently over her bottom lip "What is a day. Time ceased the moment I met you." Said he, blue eyes growing smoky. "I don't think it too soon; but if it is too soon for you then I shall try not to feel the wound too deeply and will wait until my affections are reciprocated."

She took a shaky breath she hadn't known she'd been holding, well taken in by this soulful speech. She had no wish to hurt is sensitive soul; and how could she discourage this man, he who seemed sewn from the very threads of her dreams?

"Tell me to stop." He whispered.

"I cannot." she whispered back (admittedly quite dramatically) with a small excited smile as she closed her eyes. Miranda pushed down the unease that clenched her stomach as she felt his arms encircle her, his breath brushed her lips...

A sudden shout from the path made them both jump and Miranda's heart flew into her throat. It was just children passing in their games. The solitary pair sighed and laughed with relief. After a brief moment of silence "I suppose we should head back in case they decide to bring their sport nearer us." Miranda said with heavy regret, guilt and caution finally winning over passion. She lamented internally at the ruin of what was to be her first kiss, ignoring a fleeting and unwanted feeling of relief.

He took her hand and, looking into her eyes, lifted it tenderly to his lips. "I promise you, this is not to be the end of our fun, princess." he smiled with a wink. She blushed prettily. He dropped her hand and followed her back toward the trail.

Upon stepping out of the woods Miranda began smoothing her skirts and felt Mr Kirkley gently rest a hand on her waist as he spoke quietly against her ear "How wonderful, our friends are here." She straightened to see Matthew Westbrook and Miss Cotton halted in the path looking at them in shock, and Matthew looking fit to do harm!

~~~

Matthew Westbrook and Grace Cotton, burdened upon by the heat of the sun, had taken to a trail more shaded. They had been passed by a few of children shouting loudly in their play, then a short way further Westbrook had heard a noise of something approaching the path from the brush. He paused and touched Miss Cotton's arm to halt her, worried it may be some animal, but relaxed and raised an amused eyebrow at seeing Miranda Riley come out of the woods, red cheeked and hair all askew. However, at seeing William Kirkley step out a moment after her (who stopped short as he noticed the two standing there) he could not hide his expression of shock.

Miranda was preoccupied with picking leaves from the folds of her blue day dress and hadn't yet noticed them. Kirkley, however - now smiling pointedly at Westbrook - leaned over with a hand on her waist and whispered quite familiarly in her ear. Matthew felt uncharacteristically and suddenly violent, and he urged himself not to act rashly.

"Oh!...Mr Westbrook...Miss Cotton...." Miranda began, then, feeling discomposed under Westbrook's fuming gaze, added "it's really not what it appears, we were just exploring!" Although, she thought to herself, it very nearly was exactly as it appears.

Matthew opened his mouth as if to speak, but clamped it shut as a small group of guests made up of Victoria Bradshaw, Edwin Lawrence, and
~~~

three others rounded the corner and approached them. "It seems we've interrupted something delicious" Miss Bradshaw snickered "Why don't you four join our group and share with us! We all know how to keep a secret, I know I am the soul of discretion!" She snickered again.

Westbrook smiled pleasantly "I'm sure Miss Cotton and Mr Kirkley would love to join you. I have a message to pass on to Miss Miranda, from her sister."

"We have no wish to be burdened with any secrets but our own I assure you Miss Bradshaw." Edwin Lawrence chuckled "And in my experience, it is often the case that those who claim to be discreet are by far the least so." The whole group laughed at that and they continued on towards Tenby Hall, Miss Bradshaw continuing to insist that she was most discreet and had no idea why they would think of her so unjustly.

Matthew waited for them to disappear from sight, ignoring Miranda's glares at being made to stay behind. Then, once they were out of earshot, he turned on her.

"Exploring?" Said he carefully, barely holding his frustration. "What if it had been someone other than I and Miss Cotton who had come upon the show you two just displayed?? Your actions were fodder for rumors the like of which would ruin you both! Miss Bradshaw was directly behind us, as you just beheld, and believe me she would have loved to spread all manner of elaborated stories!! Do you care so little for your reputation? Or the reputation of your partner??"

Miranda blushed severely with embarrassment. "We are not partners; we were just having a bit of fun..."

"Fun?!" Westbrook cried "It is not 'fun' to scamper about letting every charming young scamp woo you out of your virtue and besmirch the good name of your family, it is rash and thoughtless!"

Miranda glared at him in indignation, trying to squash the immense guilt he was causing her. "He is not trying to woo me out of my virtue! And I wouldn't allow him the pleasure of trying if he were! Do you truly think it is so impossible for someone to merely enjoy my company? Is your opinion of me really so low??"

"No Miranda, this isn't about the appeal of your company!" He said in exasperation "It is a matter of propriety! I want you to be cautious! If he truly cared for you, he wouldn't put your reputation at risk just for a bit of 'fun', as you call it; you deserve better than he!"

"Oh who then, someone like you??" She asked angrily, beginning to tear up "Someone who insults and scolds me at every turn?? I believe I would prefer a ruined reputation and a life full of love, over a good name and a hateful husband!" Then quickly before she could regret her hasty, passionate words she added "I have always considered you a brother, Westbrook, but I really feel you haven't the right to speak to me so regardless of how close we are!" and stormed past him embarrassed and furious. Despite copious amounts of self-justification, she knew what Westbrook had said was true.

Westbrook strode angrily down the path towards the house, rage slowly dissipating until he stopped and ran his fingers through his hair. He had been too rash; she had been correct in that he had acted in a way that was inappropriate even were he truly her brother. He could not, however, allow her to be deceived by such a man – a scoundrel he was sure – as William Kirkley; she needed someone strong-willed as she and mature, who would provide her with stability and encourage her good character, someone like....good lord he was falling for Miranda – the silly romantic who he'd always thought of as a sister, and whom he'd mercilessly teased all her life – the young woman whom he had just scolded as though she were his child. Karma had a cruel sense of humor.

~~~

The remaining days before the ending ball were torture for Westbrook. Miranda was still spending much of her time with Kirkley and, though he convinced himself he cared not, every time she entered a room his chest hurt, and when someone asked her to play on the pianoforte and sing, her voice as rich and tempting as chocolate affected him as though every ivory key she hit landed on his own heartstrings. If only her smile didn't flicker and fade every time her eyes met his. He vehemently wished he were able turn back time and stop himself from speaking to her like a father; but more so, he fancied boxing William Kirkley in his smirking face would be an famously satisfying thing to do. He was certain the man's motives were not as pure and romantic as Miranda believed.

"Ay, Matt, your turn..." Edwin Lawrence nudged him, bringing him back to reality. Lawrence glanced from Miranda to his friend, giving Westbrook a look. Westbrook mentally kicked himself for allowing his attentions to become so obvious and re-focused on the card game; after which, Lawrence took him aside for some drinks by the entrance of the sitting room and, leaning against the door jam, gave Matthew a raised eyebrow "So....? Lovers tiff?"

Westbrook looked pointedly over at where Miranda was sitting, batting her lashes at Mr Kirkley who had begun reading poetry to a small group. Miranda sat next him, fluttering her fan flirtatiously. "Does it Look like we're the lovers Lawrence? No, she did something un-ladylike and I stepped out of line and reprimanded her."

"Ah, good show Westbrook, you've really got a chance now."

"Do Shut up. I never had a chance to begin with." Matthew smirked sardonically "I have spent my life ensuring my title of brother with her and Izzy and I'm afraid I'm stuck there for good."
~~~

Lawrence smiled, "Perhaps, perhaps not. There's something off about that dandy. From the little I've talked on the subject of him with Miss Cotton it doesn't seem as though she's formed much of a good opinion of him. I get the feeling she knows him better than she lets on."

"I have noticed" Matthew confirmed "Perhaps you could take her aside some time and ask her to warn Miranda off him, if she knows something."

"You should be the one to ask her, you seem closer to her than I."

"Good lord Lawrence, take an opportunity when you're given one; I'm not the only one who isn't subtle in his conquests" Westbrook smirked.

Edwin Lawrence assessed his friend's meaning for a moment, then grinned "Damn."

Westbrook laughed "You are in a better position than I, lucky bastard."

"Aye Matt, I can hope," replied his friend, "but you've not got my sympathy, for your grave was dug by your own hand."

Chapter 8

Morning dawned on the final day of the Tenby house party. Those who lived nearby returned, bringing the number of guests steadily back up over the course of the afternoon. Isabel Riley was met with sorry news as Miss Dunsworth informed she would be leaving before the ball. Isabel cried out in dismay and begged they stay for the ball and 'could they not postpone one night?' but alas Miss Dunsworth's family had booked rooms in Bath prior to the invitation to the Tenby house party, and must claim them on the promised day.

Mrs Dunsworth and her husband, who were lounging nearby on a setee, offered a spontaneous solution to the problem of their leaving. Mr Dunsworth began. "Gracious me, you two girls are so loath to part, my wife and I do not feel right in separating you. What say you to this then, Miss Riley; if you can bear missing tonight's ball, and are not oppose to a rushed departure, we have room in our humble barouche for one more and our rooms in bath have extra bedchambers – then we may return you home on our way back to Southamptons."

Mrs Dunsworth greatly approved this plan, saying she would tell her son – who would arrive in Bath an hour ahead them – to inform the staff to prepare a room and everything would be arranged without any fuss or bother.

Isabel Riley was flustered and unsure; not that she cared for a ball over visiting Bath with a family who'd become so recently dear to her, and she did not think three hours too little time to gather some trunks – those could be sent after her of course – but she did not wish to be a burden and she worried her father would not approve. It took little convincing to satisfy her that she would be the opposite of a burden, and Sicily Dunsworth's joy at the prospect of Isabel joining them secured her.

All that was left was to speak to Lord Riley, who's good opinion of the family solidified his approval.

Miranda was far less pleased or approving and was quite angry with Isabel, who tried to calm her livid sister while also choosing gowns to bring, nearly shaking with excitement and haste.

"This is our party and our ball! You cannot be absent! You must be present to thank everyone for coming, and you will miss out on dancing, and who will I speak to while you are gone; you are abandoning me! Do you not care for your sister's comfort and happiness??"

"Oh Em, you know I love you, do not take to such dramatics. Though I feel guilty and melancholy leaving you, Love, you know I shan't be very sorry to miss tonight's ball. I have already thanked people a hundred times over for coming, I am not fond of crowds and the general overabundance of noise that follows them; I do love dancing but the positives of balls are far outweighed by the negatives in my opinion."

"Not so! In any case, you are only thinking of yourself and chasing down your splendid Mr Dunsworth. He may be the handsomest man in the room but he is still poor as a mouse and very cold-mannered."

"I am not chasing Mr Dunsworth, I genuinely love his sister and find her company preferable to anyone else's but yours! And he is not poor as a mouse, five-thousand a year is far more than enough to sustain a very comfortable living!"

"Lawd help us you are dreaming of a life with him already." Miranda scoffed derisively.

"I am not. And I don't see how you get off slighting the Dunsworths when your Mr Kirkley isn't nearly as wealthy as they!"

Miranda fumed silently, not having anything intelligent to respond with. "Why?" she said finally "What is he worth and who did you hear it from?"

"I heard from a handful of people he has two thousand or less to his name and that it is rumored he would have much more would he not gamble so often."

"I doubt you heard it from anyone reputable, most likely gossips, I don't believe he is the type to gamble."

"Oh and you know him well of course," Isabel interrupted dryly "having briefly spoken to him on three occasions, danced with him five, and fluttered your lashes at him too many times to count."

Miranda huffed at that. "I do not flutter my lashes at anyone. Some people are open and sensitive making them easier to learn than others; at least he is not so distant and cold that conversation is impossible, like your choice of man."

Isabel did not try to reason with her sister any longer. "Enough of this arguing, I do not like it. I will be back before you know it. I dare say you will enjoy the ball all the more for me being absent, for you will be free to act yourself without me constantly telling you to hold your tongue or cease flirting." Miranda began to lament again, about her sister leaving her with barely a moment's notice, but Isabel, exhausted of the discord between them, said rather unkindly "I know what this is truly about. You are no doubt furious over my being in Bath, and being invited to travel with friends, while you are to stay home."

Tears formed in Miranda's eyes; with hurting heart and ridged form she left her sister's room, slamming the door against Isabel's sincere and apologetic claim of not meaning what she said.

Miranda could not let her sister leave without a goodbye, no matter how disappointed and angry she may be. They embraced tearfully before Isabel lit into the Dunsworth's barouche.

"I still cannot believe you are so determined to leave me." Miranda clutched her sisters hands, pulling her into another embrace "I do not know how I shall ever forgive you for it." declared she.

Isabel knew no words would comfort her sister, and did not trust her own voice not to shake, so she said nothing. With one kiss placed on her sister's cheek she joined her companions and they began to move.

"Write me!" Miranda called.

"I shall!" Isabel promised. The twins waved furiously at each other until Isabel disappeared from view, and Miranda stood beside her Papa and Matthew with tears on her cheeks.

Lord Riley squeezed his daughters hand and Matthew Westbrook put a hand on her shoulder, "You will see her again soon and just imagine the stories you will have to share." said he gently, "And there is no need to be so down, you have me to play her role while you are gone." he added with a lopsided grin.

"Oh joy," was her sarcastic reply, "what a comfort." but she could not help but smile a little and feel somewhat cheered up. She straightened with a sniff and quickly wiped her cheeks with a hand, she grinned at the two beside her. "There now, I am composed, you may both breathe a sigh of relief and go about your business as usual; I have but an hour and one half to prepare for a ball and haven't a moment to waste." she turned and took herself indoors with dignified air.

The two men looked at each other with raised eyebrows, then let out a deep breath and re-entered the manor.

~~~

Miranda donned a peach gown overlaid with a sheer floral-embroidered layer of fabric. After her abigail had done up the stays in the back, she sat down to have her hair arranged. As she watched the progress on her hair she thought, as she had often the last few days, of her argument with Matthew. She recalled with regret her actions that day; though she still lamented at the ruination of what would have been her first kiss, she appreciated the truth in what Matthew had said. More so than that, however, she recalled with some confusion at the soft flutter in her chest when he had said she deserved better. He truly cared for her and Izzy, more so than any man she knew besides her father. She thought with regret her words to him, he did not ever really scold her, he was just protective of her reputation and wanted to bring out the best in her. And she was fond of his teasing, it only bothered her when caused her to fret that he might think badly of her. She should not have implied that a life of matrimony with him would be hateful for he was the best man she knew and any woman would be very happy to find herself espoused to him. She considered for a moment if she would be happy to find herself espoused to him...then told herself she was raving mad to have such thoughts about a man who cared for her as a sister, and shushed any other strange and troublesome thoughts about him.

As her lady's maid finished pulling her long hair into a cascading bun, Miranda attached her dance card to her wrist and found her father waiting
~~~

to walk with her down to the Grand Ballroom. The music started as she arrived and she quickly scanned the room for Mr Kirkley. At seeing him nearby with Victoria Bradshaw she made her way towards them. They stopped their conversation to welcome her.

Miranda smiled, "Good evening you two, I didn't mean to interrupt!"

Mr Kirkley gave her a happy smile. "On the contrary Miss Ryley. I have been in torture waiting for you to appear!" He said. Miss Bradshaw snickered.

Miranda blushed prettily "I know you merely flatter me Mr Kirkley; but here, the first dance will soon begin and I have no partner," (this predicament coming about by design as she had rejected many requests for it) "if you were to ask me to dance I may believe you are sincere." She extended her wrist and he obligingly wrote his name in a few spaces.

"Not the first?" She pouted at seeing that one still blank.

"I have promised that one to Miss Bradshaw." He explained.

They conversed pleasantly for a moment and when Victoria turned to respond to someone who spoke to her, he took Miranda's gloved fingers gently in his and drew close to whisper lightly in her ear.

"I long to hold you in my arms above anyone else but, you see, she asked me for the dance and courtesy forced me to accept." He dropped her hand as Victoria began to turn back towards them.

Miranda was surprised that the girl would be so bold and she felt a glimmer of irritation towards Miss Bradshaw. But it could not be helped. She subtly observed the room for another partner for the important 'first dance'. Seeing Edwin Lawrence speaking to Miss Cotton, who glowed in a pale pink gown, she began to approach them in hopes her cousin may save her when she felt a light tap on her shoulder.

"He has asked Miss Cotton so you won't have any luck there."

"Then it appears I don't have much choice but to hope you will ask Matthew, for there isn't anyone else I'd really care to share the first dance with." She sighed.

Matthew raised a brow. "I suppose I should be honored since there are many eligible men here, but your tone suggests an insult..."

She began to defend herself, but the band struck the starting chords and Matthew lead her to the floor to sweep her into the dance before she could decide what to say. After taking a few turns in silence Miranda finally joked "You're very quiet tonight, I've been expecting some comment on the impropriety of my actions, or the inferiority of the company I'm keeping, or that my bodice is too low."

Matthew forced his eyes to stay on her face at her last comment, "If I'm to be honest, I feel the need to beg your forgiveness Miranda. I fear I often step out of place with both my teasing and advice. I realize now I have often been unkind to you.."

Admittedly she was enjoying his apology, but at one point she could not help but interrupt "Oh I do not find you unkind!" and then with much effort muttered "No need for an apology, what you said a few days ago was not untrue." Then at his surprised expression she added "Don't get a swelled head Mr Westbrook! It is unlikely I'll be willing to admit you are right ever again!" They grinned, their relationship now mended and at ease with each other once more.

The next dance she, to her immense pleasure, was partnered with Mr Kirkley. They swayed together in silence, enjoying each other's company. She looked into his blue eyes and he drew her closer to say quietly "You are so beautiful, my princess." and cause little butterflies in her stomach.

"And you as charming a prince as any woman could dream of!" She replied prettily. With a man such as this, who treated her so well, who spoke and moved with such care and attention, who knew his own heart and did not hide from her his feelings, how could she find better? Even if the rumors were true of his little fortune, Miranda thought she might be able to sacrifice some comfort for one who really loved her, and it was clear Kirkley was falling for her. Izzy and Matthew Westbrook's opinions of Kirkley be damned, what did they know of love in any case?? She giggled aloud

"What is it?"

"Something of little consequence. You know, I have been warned against you." Laughed she.

"Ah, yes, people are always too ready to believe those things they hear from others, without considering where the information came from." His smile did not mask the sadness in his eyes.

"You know I am not so quick to judge, I form my own opinion of others upon closer acquaintance." She smiled up at him.

"And has our acquaintance grown close enough for you to form one?"

"Yes, I find you genuine, charming, and too good." Laughed she.

"Nay, not too good, I am far from it princess. I do not deserve such a high opinion as that." denied he sincerely. "There are many who could greatly diminish me in your eyes and I dread the day you look at me as they do, for I know you shall."

"Not so surely! There is no one who could sway my opinion once it is set."

"I am glad...I admit, I do not easily trust. A lady I once loved was persuaded by another's false rumors to hate me, and now I have no faith in the hearts of those who claim to love me."

"Who is this pray! How could she be so easily swayed?!"

"No matter, it is in the past; I shall try to have faith in your promise of loyalty and pray you are sincere."

Miranda said nothing, unsure of what to think. She had been confident of his character but he himself had now admitted a sullied reputation. Though she still believed him to be humbled and sincere, there was now a small doubt that he was not one she should be associating with – what if he had done something really quite bad? It was one thing to overlook one's fortune, as Izzy did, but to overlook an irreputable nature...that was another matter. No, whatever could be said against him was a product of miscommunication and elaboration; she would not be one of these ladies of fickle mind who had spread such vicious gossip and injured his kind, genuine heart!

The next dance was with an odd hook-nosed man with a stallion tail whom she recognized vaguely, and who, she realized after a few turns, thought she was Isabel. After correcting him he grew quiet and sullen. He asked where her sister was, and she obliged. He asked if her sister had a beau, and in irritation at this too-forward question she lied 'yes she does'. Then he spoke no more and seemed to forget he was dancing with someone – an intense focused look in his eyes. Miranda fled his presence as politely as possible –not that he acknowledged her – and made her way to the first familiar face in the crowd. "Matthew, I beg your attention a moment" cried she in a hushed whisper, stealing his attention from the group of older men he spoke with, clutching his arm. Once they were a little way from the crowd she asked "who was that man I just danced with, he did not give me his name and was so unpleasant and made me want to squirm!" she squirmed in disgust to accentuate her words.

"Ah, Lord Miles, he is a bit odd. Quite recently inherited a large sum after his Father and elder brother passed, poor gent; must be rough to lose a brother and then father in such quick succession."

"Ooh yes! How awful, I suppose it was unkind of me to think so ill of him so easily...but really, he does have such an disturbing air about him. I suppose no amount of money can compensate for such a loss."

"No...but has wasted no time in taking advantage of it. He has done some travelling since and is quite happily generous with it."

"Gracious, how much.."

"He is as wealthy as you I would say. Has he gained some appeal now then?" Miranda speared him with a look. "Do not be so easy to take offence, you know I jest."

She could not stay irritated at him and rolled her eyes with a smile. "We are talking into the next dance, come, ask me lest I am left without a partner."

"There is too much dancing tonight."

"Perhaps, but I know you are lively enough to handle one or two more before night's end. I wish you to dance with Miss Cotton tonight, Matthew, I don't wish her to feel left out of the festivities at any point."

"Don't fret over your Miss Cotton. Our cousin Lawrence is keeping her well entertained." he said, looking pleased.

"What??" Miranda startled, looking about to see if she could catch sight of the subjects of their conversation. Edwin Lawrence couldn't be entertaining her, she was meant for Matthew!

"What are you so distressed over?" They took to the floor as they spoke, gliding effortlessly around the room under Matthews expert lead. "Are you not thrilled to make a match of them?"

"What is your opinion of Miss Cotton Matthew? Is she not the sweetest thing? Do you not adore her?!"

"She is sweet – as you say – I suppose. She is very mature in her manner and conversation, very proper and reserved."

"Just the kind of girl for you then, as those are the qualities you always try to cultivate in me!"

He laughed. "Nay, she is too reserved and proper for my taste, I have nothing to tease or scold her about and where is the fun in that."

Miranda laughed, but it was a short laugh and she was not committed to it. It appeared Isabel was once again right, and their Mr Westbrook did not prefer meek women over lively ones. It was likely, considering how well he got on with she and Izzy, that he wished for a woman like them. The more she thought of it the more Miss Cotton seemed wrong for him and the more difficult it became for her to think of anyone she would be content to have as a sister-of-sorts, for no one was worthy of their Mr Westbrook. She and Izzy were his girls and she suddenly loathed the idea of him marrying. Miranda began to notice the strength of his arm around her waist, and her hand laying on his arm liked the feel of the muscle there. The room began to feel quite warm and her chest felt suddenly tight. She did not realize the significance of these feelings, nor realize she was now staring at him quite entranced. His lips twitched into a smile (making something in her chest twitch as well) and deep grey eyes sparked with humor.

"What on earth has you so deep in thought, Em? You are uncommonly quiet."

"Ugh!" she blushed violently "Why do you still call me that! I'm no longer a child."

"Your sister and father still call you 'Em' and you have no qualms with them."

"It is different somehow."

"I beg to differ and shan't stop"

She didn't argue further on the subject, but needing reassurance asked "You don't think it's childish?"

"Absolutely not, I will go so far as to say no one could call you anything that would make you anything less than a woman."

"Why Mr Westbrook, careful, you are waxing romantic." she grinned.

Matthew Westbrook was at that moment thinking that not only was she now a woman but a breathtaking one when Miranda's mouth fell open slightly, eyes widening as she faltered in a step; and he realized in a panic he had spoken his thought aloud!

There was silence for a heartbeat before Miranda suddenly began to laugh! "Gracious Matthew! I 'take your breath away' indeed! You really looked as though you were serious! You are an wicked tease! I say though, if you begin speaking to the opposite sex that way in earnest, you will have women dropping at your feet like flies."

He forced himself to laugh with her – making a hurried comment about having no wish to woo anyone at the present – as he struggled with both overwhelming relief and dismay. He maintained his unruffled facade until the music stopped a few seconds later and he lead her off to join Miss Cotton by the refreshments. Westbrook then immediately took himself through one of the doors leading out into the cool of the night, and let out an explosive breath. "Gads that was a close one!" Said he to the garden bushes. Then after leaning against a rail for a moment, ran his fingers through his hair, inhaled a few deep breaths, and rejoined the fray.

Chapter 9

The hours flew by with boisterous chatter and lively music. Miranda felt entirely out of sorts and utterly conflicted. Mr Westbrook's voice spoke "you take my breath away" over and over in her brain until she felt she might go mad. He was obviously joking. He must have been joking. But he had sounded so serious, eyes so sincere, it had all but stolen her breath away. She occupied her mind, trying to listen to the gossip of her friends, or think of Mr Kirkley to settle her senses. Where was he anyway?

The clock announced twelve o'clock and Miranda noticed Kirkley slip down the corridor that led to the library. Frowning at his suspicious behavior she hurried to follow; but in her rush to catch up to Kirkley, the dim hall mere steps away, she stumbled into someone who moved into her path.

"Oof! Miss Riley do watch where you are going!" Was the resulting plaintive cry.

"Ooh Miss Bradshaw, I am sorry! I was just.."

Miss Bradshaw looked peeked. "Shouldn't you be out dancing?"

"I..I have a headache, I just need to rest a moment somewhere quiet."

"Surely you can do that somewhere else."

"It is my home, I suppose I can rest wherever I wish can I not?" replied she, irritated at Miss Bradshaw's persistence in detaining her.

"Are you going to the library? That seems an odd place to rest, you should rest in your room, surely that would be more comfortable." Miss Bradshaw resorted to considerate coaxing.

"Thank you, Miss Bradshaw, for your concern" Miranda smiled a little insincerely, "but I do not need a lengthy nap, I only require a short sit-down in my favorite reading chair. Do hope you are enjoying the ball." and she turned and ventured down the hall. At the library door she looked to see Miss Bradshaw watching quite perplexed – but the girl whipped around and left once Miranda looked at her.

Miranda tentatively stepped in, closing the door quietly behind her. William Kirkley was perched on the edge of an armchair, drumming his slim fingers on the surface of a side table. The moonlight caused his golden hair to shine, giving him an ethereal blue glow. He really was quite beautiful in this light, one would almost call him handsome. He looked up with a smile and a 'hello love' as she walked towards him, then jumped slightly as his eyes met hers and a startled look flashed across his face before hiding quickly behind a mask of charm.

"Miranda; what brought you here?"

The lack of light and fog of fancy discouraged her good sense and she thought nothing of this strange reaction to her appearance. Miranda merely raised a brow and responded to his question with only a very little suspicion. "A better question is what brought you here."

"A hope" she received a joyful smile "that you would see me leave and follow, a foolish romantic notion I thought but.." He rose and came to her, taking her hands in his own "maybe not so foolish...I am so glad you've come, you are even more beautiful in the moonlight."

Miranda's meager suspicion was promptly forgotten as he caused her cheeks to flush and the now-familiar butterflies to flutter "How could I not follow my prince?" She said with a giggle, entwining their fingers. "I never turn up a nose to mystery and intrigue."

"Ah yes, I do endeavor to intrigue." laughed he. "Your mystery, however, is solved; I was waiting for you."

"But is there intrigue, Mr Kirkley? I do not see it." she tried to tease but it came out more real than she intended.

"Call me Will, Love." he merely smiled, as he ran his fingers up her neck to cup her cheek; then speaking as if to himself, "Never have I felt such a strong and fast affection, how will I bear to leave you tomorrow."

"Oh, Will," she cried in dismay, "How could you remind me of it! You needs must lend me your London address that I may write you. What excitement shall I have when you are gone? None at all!" Miranda pouted.

"We shall write, and I shall try my best to provide you with as much excitement as anyone can with pen and paper." He chuckled, then becoming sober said softly "I am glad though, to have you alone one last time." And drew her closer with one hand hot on her back, a finger slipping under her chin. "May I..princess.."

Miranda was all excitement. She wrapped her arms around him and closed her eyes, heart hammering in anticipation of her first kiss. He tipped her face up a little, and the library door creaked open.

Shoving away from Kirkley, Miranda attempted to regain composure, facing the dark figure in the doorway. She heard Kirkley hiss quietly through his teeth "That imbecile has the worst timing! Could he not have waited a half hour!"

Miranda stood in frustration and despair, unsure of what to say or do; she was on the brink of ruination! Then, to her complete alarm, Kirkley walked across the room, past the intruder, and out the door; leaving her on her own to explain the why she was alone with a man in a dark room!

As the intruder walked into the moonlit room she was both utterly relieved and thoroughly distressed to see it was Matthew Westbrook. "I suppose I should be grateful to see it is once again you who have found me in a compromising situation" she grumbled, slumping into an chair with an elbow on the chair-arm. She leaned her head on her fingers, ready for a scolding. "Are you going to reprimand me now?"

"No."

Her eyes moved to where he was standing and her heart skipped a full beat. Dark hair falling into his smoldering grey eyes, he struck an impressive figure outlined by the light of the moon; delightfully muscular, from wide shoulders to narrow hips where his hands rested. She gulped, a funny sensation rising pleasantly in her tummy. How had she never before noticed how shockingly attractive Matthew Westbrook was??

"What then? Wh-Why?" She squeaked.

He gestured for her to get up. "You have enough sense to know already what I would say to you. Come let us return to the party. "

"Why are you in the library?" She grumbled guiltily, rising from her chair.

"I saw you leave. After a few minutes I notice Kirkley was missing as well. It seemed suspicious, so I investigated."

She made a little angry face at him and as she stormed past him muttered, "Nosy. For all you know he was about to propose!" before sweeping out the door. She didn't get far however, for she had barely stepped into the empty hall when Matthew's arm slid around her waist, pulling her close against the door.

"What are you doing, hypocrite?! What is this if not compromising!?" She exclaimed, attempting to bat and push him away.

Matthew leaned his head over hers, violently whispering "Sshhhh!" Causing her to cut off her protestations with a hiccup. She clamped her mouth shut and stared at him with widening eyes as she processed his grey-green eyes so close to her own; how strong his arm felt around her waist. The hall felt suddenly warm and her heart skipped a solid beat for the second time in his presence that night.

"What do you mean he was proposing! You've known him a week!"

"I never said he was; and it matters not that it's been but a week, he has a sensitive and passionate soul which is something rare in a man and not something I'm inclined to pass up!" "But are you sure it is genuine? Are you sure he truly cares for you Em? Has he never done anything to make you question his sincerity?"

There was a long minute of silence. She pressed a hand on his chest with the feeble intent to push him away; but with her eyes settling on his lips, she had a sudden urge to do something much different.

"Do you intend to accept him if he does propose?" He asked urgently, frustrated at her lack of response. "This isn't one of your novels, Em, you must be sure! I can't watch you marry someone you don't truly love, or who doesn't care for you as he should."

Miranda struggled to remember what they were talking about but she was currently more focused on the feel of his heart beneath her hand. She placed her other hand on his chest as well, moving her fingers slightly over the fabric of his waistcoat, her mind a-whirl. Gracious his chest is solid! What does he do in his free time?! The hall was unbelievably hot and stuffy, it was becoming difficult to breath! I must tell papa to look into the ventilation in this area of the house she decided.

"You look like a gaping fish! Would you please speak woman??" Matthew spoke sharply, entirely exasperated at her lack of cooperation, and desperate to make her stop touching his chest the way she was.

Miranda snapped back to reality with an "Ouf!" of disgust and slapped his shoulder with her dance card "I've no mind to accept anyone in my first week you dunce!" before quickly making her escape into the press of partygoers.

Matthew watched her trot away and expelled a breath he hadn't realized he'd been holding, shoving his fingers through his mop of black hair. For a moment he thought she had been about to kiss him; and he'd nearly lost his senses and obliged her! He knew her opinion of him. He knew his place as a friend and brother. Still, he'd nearly been sick when she'd spoken of a proposal. Westbrook winced at the pain in his chest that accompanied the memory, sending a glare of frustration in the direction she had disappeared. He had no wish to love her as he did, it gained him only stress and misery. He rubbed the spot where the feel of her soft warm hands still lingered, before stalking out into the cool night air for the second time that night.

Chapter 10

- -

The chatter of the crowd was far too loud. The clock struck out the time with one ear-shattering bong that rattled Miranda's already strained nerves. Standing in a quieter corner of the packed great hall with Miss Cotton, she rubbed her fingers against her temple and let out a quiet groan. Her companion gave a little sigh. "It is a bit tiresome, all this noise. I shall miss my friends upon leaving tomorrow, especially you miss Riley, but I shan't miss the hubbub or the crowd."

"I can't agree more. We won't miss each other too much though I hope, for we will write, no?"

"Without a doubt!" Miss Cotton then smiled teasingly "Although I'm certain you won't have much time with all the replies to potential suitors' you will have to write!"

"Gracious I am not the only one who shall be swamped with calling cards once the week is over!" Miranda poked her friend with her fan playfully. "As for me, I shall merely ignore them! I only have one suitor I care to reply too!"

"Surely not, I am not nearly the catch you are." Miss Cotton blushed delicately before inquiring, "Who is this mystery man, I am sorry to say I may already know but I do hope I am incorrect.."

"Why Mr Kirkley of course." Then, recalling her short escapade with him a few hours earlier, exclaimed "Oh but I didn't get his address!"

"It is no matter and, in any case, we know he has yours, as he is here."

"Of course you are right, he must have thought of that, but I will ask him next I see him." She craned her neck in all directions to pick him from the crowd.

Miss Cotton spoke tentatively "Miss Riley...I hope you do not think this out of place or unwelcome...but I would caution you not to grow too close to Mr Kirkley. He has the reputation of a rake in London and I.."

Miranda waved off her friend's warning "Oh you are too sensible to believe in such gossip!" She laughed "I love you dearly so any concern you feel for me could never be taken as out-of-place or unwelcome. Fear not though Grace, it is obvious to all he has only had eyes for me this entire week, and a true rake would be a notorious flirt!" Then with a playful smile "I know you, Izzy, and Matthew would tease me wickedly if I mentioned love at first sight, but I shall mention it so cringe all you like; he has told me he loves me on more than one occasion and love is not an easy word to say."

"It is too easy a word for those who use it for their own personal gain," Miss Cotton said kindly, then continued hesitantly "and I must tell you Miranda, I know him better than I admit, he and I.."

"Miss Cotton! Oh Miss Ryley!!" A shrill voice called to them making the girls jump, they looked over to see a tittering Victoria Bradshaw pushing her way through the crowd towards them.

"I am so sorry Grace!" Miranda quietly excused herself "I really feel I must rest my head and I can bear no more silly conversation tonight!" Miss Cotton nodded in sympathy before turning to greet Miss Bradshaw. Miranda made her escape away from the clamor and up to her room, the final strains of music and voices silenced behind her closed door.

Collapsing on her bed, her mind began running over the evening's events despite her desperate attempts to rest. She was curious about what Miss Cotton had been about to say. She was slightly worried about why Kirkley had acted so strangely tonight. Most of all she was confused about why she had acted so strangely tonight!

Her mind had utterly betrayed her when Matthew had stopped her in the hall a few hours earlier. What on earth had possessed her to touch him in such an intimate way, and to nearly kiss him??...Kiss Matthew!? She chewed on the idea, thinking of the teasing sparkle that was so often in his eyes and that adorable lopsided grin...she snickered to herself; perhaps it wasn't such an unpleasant idea...

No! She shook her head, shocked and disgusted with her fancies; especially once remembering his oh-so-romantic comment about her looking like a fish. Just imagine if his annoying, fishy, honorary sister had actually tried to kiss him! He'd have blushed to rival the sunrise and never spoken to her again! She laughed; perhaps she should have tried - then he would have let her out of his iron grip and stopped interrogating her.

No, she did not feel for him in any way other than a dear friend or love him any more than one would a brother.

Miranda sobered, considering his words. Had Kirkley ever done anything to make her question his sincerity? She thought of Kirkley's confusion at seeing her enter the library, as if he had, in actuality, been waiting for someone specific; recalled him leaving her in the room alone so suddenly to explain her actions to a stranger; thought of Miss Cotton's warning...

but before she could worry herself too much more, she brushed off her fears.

He had explained his reaction, and he obviously saw who was in the doorway before she did and knew Matthew was trustworthy. As for Miss Cotton's warning, she knew it was all just gossip. She could not let the doubts and talk of others sway her from what she felt was real. Her thoughts slowly became fuzzy as her drowsiness grew.

She thought with some mild disappointment that she had still not acquired his address. She would have to hope to get it on the morrow. Sleep overtook her.

~~~

Miranda woke up the next morning significantly earlier than the rest of the house. Though considering she had also gone to bed earlier than the rest it was no surprise. Her lady's maid must have woken her at some point to help her out of her gown, she vaguely remembered the intoxicating relief that accompanied the removal of her blasted corset. After looking out the window at the risen sun with a stretch, she untangled herself from her blankets to splash her face in the wash basin. She donned a blue-and-white striped walking dress, wrapped herself in a thin shawl, and quietly made her way out to the back garden to enjoy the mid-morning sun.

After wandering contentedly through the expansive rows of floral beds and well-trimmed bushes for a time, she came upon her current favorite spot – a trickling stream fell pleasantly over rocks and pebbles and into a small pond. A pond which was currently home to a mother duck and seven fluffy ducklings. Miranda set herself on a stone bench nearby to watch the ducklings be taught how to dive for minnows; tails and webbed feet poking out of the water as they dunked their heads underwater, tiny wings and head flicking off water as they popped back up. She grinned and
~~~

laughed silently as she watched, until she heard the crunch of boots on gravel behind her.

With the excited and meager hope of it being Mr Kirkley, she turned eagerly to greet him. It was not Mr Kirkley...

Chapter 11

Mr Westbrook strode leisurely into her view, not noticing her at first, which gave her a brief moment to take in his sleepy appearance. Coat unbuttoned and white shirt undone at the neck, hair poking up all askew, a slight shadow of morning stubble decorating his jaw. Her heart did a flip-flop for some strange and unnatural reason. He finally looked up then and halted his walk when he noticed her, smoky eyes meeting her own. She blushed violently, her mind helpfully recalling her thoughts last night regarding Matthew and kisses. She struggled to shoo away her unbidden memories and maintain composure.

"Em?" He blinked

"M-Mr Westbrook...what are you doing up? It's only half past ten."

He quirked up a brow at her use of his surname. "I could sleep no longer, I had much on my mind." He scratched the back of his head as he walked over to sit with her "Why are you up at this hour? Everyone else will be abed for another hour or two yet."

"I claim a restless mind as well." Miranda sympathized. "And I did retire earlier than the rest."

"Mhmm" he gazed sleepily at the antics of the ducklings, seemingly deep in thought. He looked so adorably somnolent and boyish she couldn't help but let a bubble of laughter escape, making him glance at her with eyebrow raised.

"What's got your spirits so heightened this morning?"

"I don't often get the pleasure of seeing you so rumpled."

"Pfft! I wasn't expecting to meet anyone but the ducks and fish! It can't be helped."

She shook her head with an uncontainable grin and changed the subject. "You will be staying for supper once everyone has departed, I assume?"

He looked to her...turned back to the pond "It was not my plan, but as you extended the invitation..."

"Lies, you were waiting for the invitation; nay, I correct myself, you were not waiting for an invitation for you know you do not need one and were planning on invading regardless." She laughed.

"You would be correct any other day, but I leave for London tomorrow early, so I was planning on heading back to the estate before making the journey. I will be away there on business for some time."

"Oh, then no! you must go, you would be too pressed for time if you stayed for supper, and we would not wish to inconvenience you! I am sorry you will be leaving so soon though, after having just returned home, how long will you be away?"

"Eight or ten weeks probably. At least. And it would not be of any inconvenience, but as much as I would love to stay and dine with the family this evening, I really should start off early."

"Heavens that's an unfortunate stretch of time! What business is it that would keep you away from us so long?" She asked, dismay settling too heavily in her chest and showing on her face.

He flicked a curious glance her way "I am securing myself a terrace in Town. The location is very clean and quiet and it is a very agreeable size, for a terrace. I am planning some renovations for it and I must be there to oversee said renovations. It is proving to be more of a hassle than I anticipated." He sighed, combing some hair into place with his fingers.

"Oh yes you have mentioned this endeavor. It is convenient to have a place of your own in Town of course, but I think it a sorry thing as now you will be encouraged to quit Thornhill more frequently and then when shall we see you!"

With a chuckle he teased "I did not imagine my extended absence was something you would consider 'a sorry thing'. Shall you miss my scolding and taunting?"

Miranda laughed "We are used to seeing you at least once a week, how could your presence not be missed?" then more seriously, "You do scold and taunt like anything, and I know I do over-react in response to it; but rest assured, Matthew, nothing could diminish my love for you," she placed a hand on his arm with sincere gaze, stopping his heart, "you are my dearest friend next to Izzy you know; you could not be dearer were you truly our brother."

Matthew gave a strangled laugh running fingers through his hair in agitation, looking to the sky, then turned his head away from her, appearing to focus very hard on a passing peacock. After a short few seconds he stood abruptly "I should make myself presentable before the house wakes." He reached up to tip his hat in valediction, and finding no hat there, quickly combed his hair with his fingers again. He spun around to face the way he had come, and in surprisingly few strides was gone.

Miranda sat staring at the tall bushes he had vanished behind, confounded by his sudden odd departure and feeling annoyingly hollow in his absence. "Was it something I said?" She jokingly asked mama duck, then, in order to speak her thoughts aloud "I beg your wise input my feathered friend, what fine qualities drew you to Mr Mallard? Did he romance you and excite you, or did he make you warm and comfortable and tingly inside? And which one of those are symptoms of love?" Wait, love? Miranda inquired of herself with some surprise, then quietly aloud, "Am I falling in love with Matthew Westbrook??"

Mama duck blinked and bobbed her head.

"Is there any other explanation for the emotions and reactions he pulls from me of late? It cannot be familial affection, I am used to feeling that with him. But what of Will Kirkley, I am so certain I am falling in love with him!" She groaned and put her head in her hands feeling a headache beginning again.

Mama duck shook her head and ducked underwater.

"I shall just have to wait and see which one grows and lasts. Surely whatever passing attraction I have for Matthew will fade. Will is everything I want in a man, everything I have dreamed of since I was old enough to think of men."...But her assurance to herself felt empty, and every time she envisioned William Kirkley's enchanting blue eyes, a pair of teasing grey-green ones made them fade from her mind.

Mama duck paddled in a circle and quacked helpfully.

Miranda sighed, shrugging her slipping shawl further up her shoulders. "All too unfortunate I do not speak waterfowl." She muttered, then after a few contemplative minutes stood and smoothed her skirts, following the path back to the Manor. The house party was over, and in a short hour and a half the last of the guests would be packing carriages and heading home;

and with them would go Mr Westbrook and Mr Kirkley. Her confused and exhausted brain both mourned their impending departure and bid them both an exasperated adieu. She wished desperately her Izzy were here with her.

~~~

Those who had the farthest to travel were the first to leave, and so it was that Miranda bid a teary goodbye to Miss Cotton and cousin Charity Bertram at midday. Mr Kirkley left shortly before lunch, they had no time at all to steal away alone, so she forced herself to be content with the subtle kiss he brushed over her fingers.

"You never prepared me your address, William. You will write me will you not?" She urged him

"Most definitely princess," he assured and with a quick smile he turned, mounted his horse, and rode off. She implored him silently to look back at her; but he did not, and with a resigned sigh she watched him turn the bend and disappear.

The dinner bell rang, calling Miranda (and the twenty-six guests that remained) in for late lunch. She sat by her aunt during the meal, listening to conversation that surrounded railways, parliament, and updates on the declaration of war on France. Miranda tried to listen and for it was good to stay informed of news outside of her own circles (the talk of war was quite worrisome); but such heavy talk was immensely boring, despite her best efforts to find it otherwise, and she often caught her mind wandering.

A cough woke her from her absent-minded doldrums and her eyes refocused to see Matthew Westbrook a few seats down opposite her, fist in front of his mouth, looking at her with a raised brow and the corner of his mouth twitching with quiet laughter. She realized she had been staring into the space between them, spoon half raised, for quite possibly
~~~

a full minute; her dessert had even fallen off the useless silver utensil and onto the table in front of her plate. She felt her cheeks burn at being caught in such an awkward state and wiped away the chocolate blob with a kerchief, praying no one else had observed her graceless behavior, though that was unlikely. Bending over her little crystal dessert bowl, she focused determinedly on it for the rest of the meal. Every once in a while, during the rest of the meal, she would meet the eye of Mr Westbrook; every time, he would have a mischievous glint there, and every time, she blushed and laughed internally - embarrassed anew.

After lunch Miranda met him outside to bid him farewell and safe journey.

"I haven't yet had the chance to commend you on your table manners Em! I have never seen a more elegant and graceful lady, I am utterly taken!" he grinned, taking her hand to bow over it.

She let out a groan but grinned, "Do not remind me! I was hoping you would not recall it, for I knew you would never allow me to forget it!"

"You know me well enough not to have such fruitless hopes!"

"Ouf!" She laughed, "some days I wish I knew you less!"

His leather-clad fingers moved slightly on her palm with his responding laughter, sending warm shivers up her arm and bringing her to the realization he still held her hand. She tugged her fingers gently from his light grasp and he quickly let go, rubbing his hand on his breeches. He said goodbye to her parents one last time and swung onto his great black horse in one smooth motion. 'Such a natural daily action, yet he does it so well' Miranda observed with satisfaction; then internally rolled her eyes at such silly thoughts. He trotted away and, as he reached the bend in the roadway, turned to lift a hand at them...Miranda smiled and waved before he turned back and rode out of sight. The annoying hollow feeling from the morning returned.

There were few others to send off and in less than an hour Tenby Hall was empty once more but for Lord Riley and Miranda.

Chapter 12

Bath itself could not lay claim to all the joy and contentment of Isabel Riley, no matter how beautiful and exciting it deigned to be. She had been to the town before, and though she still greatly enjoyed her rare trips there, it had lost the appeal of being a new place with much to see and explore. Isabel's joy came from being a guide and host-of-sorts for the Dunsworths as it was their first time in Bath. She had some acquaintance there which helped at parties and dinners as she could introduce them.

She took them to the Grand Pump Room first thing the day after they arrived, as it was considered the place to be and must be visited before anything else on any given day, they determined it was a beautiful and lively place but that as there was little to do there in the morning and early-afternoon besides hope to bump into an acquaintance they found it rather over-rated. The third day they went shopping for bathing gowns and spent the evening at a concert at the Pump Rooms.

The fourth day they visited the Roman Baths early when there would be few others there. Isabel was the quickest to change and waited contentedly in the warm waters for the other four to arrive. She floated on her back, eyes closed, until someone pushed her shoulder. "Oh I am sorr..oh!" It was Eugene Dunsworth, and he was (as could be expected) in a bathing suit.

"h-hello." She stuttered, blushing hard. It is a bathing suit, Isabel, there is no need to blush so! Thought she to herself in exasperation. She wished she could attempt some sort of conversation, but really should not, as there was no chaperone present. Sicily Dunsworth took all too long in coming, and when she finally did – arm in arm with Mrs Dunsworth and followed by Mr Dunsworth Sr – Isabel let out a sigh of relief.

"Miss Dunsworth come in, the water is splendid!" called she, and when accompanied by her friend added quietly "but where are your stockings dearest! You cannot bathe with your legs and feet bared for the men to gawk at!"

"Gracious it is only my ankles; I do not see the fuss. Men do not gawk at ankles."

"They do!"

"They don't. Eugene is a man, let us ask him!"

"No don't!" Isabel cried, but Miss Dunsworth was already doing so.

"What say you Eugene? Do you gawk at ankles??"

"I do not gawk at anything, whether it be ankles or elbows or a fine set of Friesians." he obliged dryly.

"How peculiar..." Isabel muttered with amusement.

"Which is peculiar;" Sicily questioned mirthfully, "that my brother compared elbows to horses, or that he does not gawk."

"I never considered him one to gawk."

With humor playing on her lips, Sicily raised her brows at her brother who merely stared back at her without expression.

"I was not comparing; I was merely explaining I do not gawk at anything."

"Right; well I cannot say I agree." and she dunked herself underwater before her brother could demand her meaning. Isabel sunk down to her chin, relishing the feel of the water on her skin. Sicily popped back up. "How do you feel about this crush we are to attend tonight Miss Riley? Do you wish to go?"

Isabel was unsure how to respond, so she did so honestly yet also considerate of her friends wanting to go. "I am never full of energy after a swim, but I'm sure it will be enjoyable enough."

"There, see? I told you she would not wish to go." Sicily directed this at her brother triumphantly, who grumbled about his sister not being discrete in the least.

"I did not say so!" Isabel corrected quickly, "I do not want to deter you if you are looking forward.."

"You do not wish to go, but are being polite." her friend interrupted with this deduction. "My brother and I would rather not go out tonight, especially after bathing, but he insisted we must go as you would wish to!"

"Gracious no, I will always prefer to remain in a comfortable place with those I am comfortable with. Do not feel as though you must suffer yourselves for my sake!"

"If you are sure you would prefer it.." Eugene watched her.

"Oh I would. Miranda is forever angry with me for being such a home-body." she admitted.

"Isabel, who is that man who watches us so obviously?" Miss Dunsworth's gaze was focused behind her friend. "I noticed him in the pump room yesterday as well.." but as Isabel turned to look, "Ah, never mind, he is gone." and turning back around, Isabel was doused in the face by a wall of water. "Eugene!" Sicily cried, "Poor, Miss Riley; how could you!"

A bewildered Isabel blinked, looking from Miss Dunsworth's exuberant face to Mr Dunsworth's indignant and irritated one. "I did not.." he began, but received a mouthful of water due to his sister directing another wave of water his way. To Isabel's glee Mr Dunsworth attacked Sicily, and the three of them began splashing each other wildly until Mrs Dunsworth was assaulted by accident and demanded they act like the adults they were.

~~~

Fire crackled and snapped in the hearth that gray and rainy evening, and Isabel sat with Mr and Mrs Dunsworth playing a game of cards. Sicily Dunsworth sat swaddled under quilts entranced in a gothic novel, her brother sat opposite reading a novel of his own – much less gothic.

The game ended with Mrs Dunsworth the winner, and Isabel skipped over to throw herself gracefully next to Miss Dunsworth on the chaise, glancing at the title of her friend's volume. "'Castle of Otranto'...Oh that is an old one. You and my sister should share a reading list, she loves a good gothic. I can't say I care for them much."

"Hmm, they are fascinating." Miss Dunsworth muttered non-committally, utterly engrossed in her tale.

"You will not succeed in gaining her attention for the next two or three hours." Eugene Dunsworth informed. "She will be dead to the world until she finishes her book, and woe to the poor soul who tears her away from it before then."

"Heavens. An avid reader then." Isabel replied with playful sarcasm. "As you are not so intimidating as your sister with a book in hand, I shall impose upon you; what do you read, Mr Dunsworth?"

"I read a history of Caligula. Not so interesting as Radcliffe or The Monk."
~~~

"Any man who makes his horse a consul could never be considered less interesting than a fiction of any genre."

"You have read it??" Mr Dunsworth grinned, the first time she had ever seen him do so. Isabel was elated.

"Why yes! It is in papa's library, of course."

"You have an extensive one at Tenby I assume."

"We have two or three. Our biggest library is larger than most I suppose. It is quite old, it has not been updated since long before we were born, and there are a great many books one must wear gloves to read – and read ever so gently. I have not touched that section for fear of ruining them."

"Fascinating!" Mr Dunsworth breathed, looking very fascinated indeed.

"Well next time you are at Tenby you must remind me to give you a tour of it."

"I thank you, I will." He grinned again "I did not think you would be interested in history."

"You also believed I would wish to attend a crush over spending a quiet evening alone with friends. You are expert at forming incorrect assumptions Mr Dunsworth."

"All the world is, Miss Riley, you cannot fault me for it."

"I can, but I would be a hypocrite for doing so." she smiled.

"That is fair. But my assumptions are not baseless, you and your sister seemed to enjoy dancing a great deal when I saw you at Tenby."

"Oh, well, I do love dancing; It is just...I am not over-fond of too many people gathered in once place. I have never been to a true crush before but I do not like the sound of it."

"A pity – in striving to avoid the disadvantages of a ball you miss out on the joys of it."

Isabel laughed. "It is true; but Miranda and I often dance together at home. Our governess would play for us when we were young, and papa plays a little now. Does Mrs Dunsworth play pianoforte? Then I could dance with Sicily and there would be no loss in staying in tonight."

Mrs Dunsworth had been eavesdropping from where she sat with her needlework. "I play moderately well, Miss Riley, but Eugene has warned you off disturbing our Sicily from her novel and I would heed his advice." Sicily glanced up briefly at hearing her name, but that was the extent of her contribution to the conversation.

"Ah, it cannot be helped then." sighed Isabel. "I shall have to bear a night without dancing." Joked she. The fire crackled in the contented quiet for a few moments.

"If mother played, I would not be opposed to a dance or two." Eugene offered gallantly.

Isabel could have cried with joy, until she recalled the last time they danced together, then she blushed hard and claimed she could not for she was a poor dancer.

"I have danced with you before," Eugene reminded her, plunging her deeper into mortification for she had hoped he had forgotten. "you are not a poor dancer; I declare you are displaying false modesty."

Isabel stared at him. "And I declare you are displaying a too generous amount of kindness, for I recall I danced very ill and you had to save me."

Mr Dunsworth smiled "I am not merely being kind, honest; I considered you the best partner I had that night."

"Then all the women in attendance must have been in very poor form, I pity you Mr Dunsworth."

"Am I playing or am I not?" begged Mrs Dunsworth, unsure whether to set down her project or not.

"If you would be so kind, mother." Mr Dunsworth stood, and his mother set aside her needlework to move to the instrument.

"Oh very well." Isabel gave in begrudgingly, yet also with immense pleasure, and took his proffered hand.

Mrs Dunsworth began to play. "This is a pretty tune, Mrs Dunsworth, you play more than moderately well!" Isabel observed gleefully.

"What is this noise!" Miss Dunsworth cried from the pages of her novel, "I cannot hear myself think!"

"So remove yourself to your room then!" Mr Dunsworth Sr offered.

That night Isabel wrote to her sister. I hope you have forgiven me now, Em, love. Fear not that I will fill this missive with all the parties I have attended and gentlemen I have swooned over with the intent of inciting jealously in you, for I have done neither in the four of five days I have been in Bath. You will be disappointed to hear I am thoroughly enjoying a relaxing and very boring time with the Dunsworths doing very little indeed. Wednesday, we arrived and went straight to our rooms. Thursday, we visited the pump room for two hours and I introduced them to Mr and Mrs Brandt – who used to live near us if you recall and vacation in Bath every summer and Autumn – who we met there by happy accident, and now the Dunsworth's have two more acquaintance here; we then attended a dinner at the Brandts that evening. Friday we visited the pump room one hour, toured the roman baths for two, and then went shopping for bathing gowns; friday evening was spent at a very lively modern concert. Today we visited the roman baths to swim and remained there all afternoon until we were shriveled like anything. We were meant to attend a crush tonight but the general consensus was we were all very worn out and wished to stay in – so we did. Miss Dunsworth, like you, is a great lover of gothics and thrilling adventures; it has been made clear to me that she does not appreciate being disturbed while reading, so Mr and Mrs Dunsworth and her brother are forced to entertain me when she finds herself a novel. Mr Eugene Dunsworth insisted I dance with him tonight while his mother played, it was loads of fun, I am perfectly, perfectly happy! Almost one week of three is over and I do not wish to think of it! Tell me what I missed of our second ball, oblige my curiosity; did you dance often with your famous Mr Kirkley? How is papa? How is Matthew? Give them both my love, And to you I give the most love! Your Izzy

Chapter 13

Izzy! How angry I am you were not with me that night! I have much to tell you and I need your advice for you were always wiser than me, sister. Let me first summarize the ball: I danced the first with Matthew (you may rest now that Matthew's first dance with me has been redeemed, think badly of me no longer), but I danced with Kirkley for the second. It was lovely, naturally. You know what I have always wanted in a husband, and he is exactly that vision: gallant, romantic, handsome and elegant; but now I must admit I feel a little unconvinced of his affections. He did not deny his questionable reputation when it came up in conversation during the dance; and another thing, I saw Kirkley sneak off into the library late into the ball. I followed of course, as is it not strange for him to sneak away to an empty room in the middle of a party in our own home? He claimed he was waiting for me, but it does not seem likely does it? He has mostly convinced me of his intentions in retreating there, and he was ever so romantic that I very nearly secured a kiss had Matthew not discovered us (I know you are shocked and will reprimand me for being so willing but hush and read on). He left! Matthew entered, and before we were able to tell who it was, Kirkley left! It distresses me he may be less than what he seems, but I am becoming more inclined to think less of him.

Carrying on with my tale – Matthew refrained from scolding me, shockingly, and I (being irritated at the time; he did foil my first kiss) might have told him his nosy behavior might have ruined a proposal (which is so preposterous I thought he would respond in jest) and he acted very strangely. He was very earnest in discouraging my acceptance (ridiculous), and circumstances apparently required him to hold me quite close, and (Allow me to assure you that it is difficult and uncomfortable for me to continue writing, knowing whom I write of) I had the thought that he is incredibly handsome and caring and I had very strange feelings I can't name – I say Izzy, I felt the urge to kiss him! Our Matthew! It is to strange to even think about! He and I also met by chance in the gardens the following morning (quite obnoxiously early, I could not sleep). He was very rumpled and sleepy and I have come to believe I may be developing feelings for him; but surely that cannot be! I know not what to think. I require your input.

Oh, another odd thing: I accepted a dance with a one Lord Miles. He was the gentleman who shunned Miss Dunsworth's company to seek yours that first night, do you recall? He thought I was you, naturally, for the first half of the dance, and when corrected he demanded to know your whereabouts and began asking very forward questions; he asked if you had a beau! I told him you did. I did not like him in the least, a snake-ish sort of man.

I am glad you are enjoying Bath and the company of your companions. I can't believe you would forgo a crush for lagging about in your rooms, for shame, I should have gone to bath in place of you for you are wasting the city's delights. Now for the greatest news! I was invited by cousin Charity to join she and Bertram in London! I am to journey to them in three days' time and spend the remainder of the season in Town! I could not be happier except you were there with me – perhaps you may join me there when you are quit Bath. I look forward to your response with great anticipation sister, do please address it to cousin Charity's terrace on Whitehall street.

The most love,

Your Em

Chapter 14

Miranda, dearest, you absolutely must re-think your vision of an ideal match; handsome looks, elegance, and charm are qualities found in every rake in England! How could your thoughts move so quickly from suspicion to supplication?? I am disappointed in you, meeting men you have just met in dark rooms alone is begging for something terrible to happen, I am glad Matthew found you. I agree it does not seem likely he was waiting for you; I would dare say it is more likely he was waiting for someone else and you surprised him! And to leave you alone and not deign to protect you or your honor...what if it had not been Matthew who found you? What a dissolute character, I dearly hope you were thoroughly put off of him after that scene and are now no longer in danger of harboring any feelings for him!

After much consideration I have decided to congratulate you on your newfound feelings for our Mr Westbrook. I was in disbelief at first, but now I have thought on it for some time I have come to the following conclusion: Matthew Westbrook is far superior to every other man you have claimed to love. He is not stupid, he is not rash or indecent, he is well settled, and quite the most handsome man of our acquaintance. If a difference in age of eleven years is not too horrid an idea, I think you would do well to love him. In any case, he has always been part of our family so it only seems proper to make it official.

As for wasting the city's delights, I beg to differ and declare I am experiencing every one of the delights Bath could offer me. Rest assured, sister dear, I have attended a crush since I sent you a letter last; you may have found it enjoyable and I wish you many a crush once you are in London. I did not find it enjoyable being pushed about and squashed between bodies at every turn – I am certain some men used it to their advantage in order to take liberties, my bottom and arms and waist were 'accidently' fondled one to many a time. Sicily complained of the same and so Mr Eugene Dunsworth was most gallant in remaining behind us when we took it upon ourselves to venture into the crowd, the amount of fondling decreased when he was with us. My affection for him has increased yet more; I did not think it possible.

It is a shocking scary thing hearing your account of Lord Miles as he was here at the pump rooms yesterday afternoon. He was staring at Sicily and I from across the room, not coming to greet us or moving his gaze from us for even a moment, and caused us such discomfort we left in haste! I almost wish you had not told me for now I will be loath to leave our rooms lest I encounter him again. I am sure he is merely odd and perfectly harmless, I'm sure it is a coincidence he is in Bath; I laugh...but in my heart I do not think it funny.

I am thrilled you are now in London sister! It is so much more the place to be than Bath for the season. We are to remain two more weeks. I will write to papa and ask him if I may join you there once I am quit Bath. I wait in heavy anticipation for your responding letter,

The most love,

Your Izzy

Chapter 15

I am so sorry I am so long in writing back to you! I knew you would scold me about the library debacle. The more I think of Kirkley's behavior the more I am unsure of him. He has not written me once since he departed, after assuring me so prettily he would. Surely if he had sent a letter home it would have been re-directed here by now; I have been here over a week after all! Town is absolutely lovely! Yesterday we visited Almack's where I found dear Miss Cotton. Grace says she sees him at most functions but never at Almacks's, which is not surprising as I doubt he would be able to acquire a voucher if the rumors of his financial state are true. I hope I shan't see him while I am here, I am determined to be a picture of discretion and propriety from this moment on. Grace says our Mr Westbrook has not attended any functions to her knowledge, but that Cousin Edwin is in town. I regret to inform Grace will not do for Matthew, I feel she is affectionate towards Cousin Edwin and Matthew inferred once at our coming out that Edwin may also fancy her.

I had told myself yesterday I shall not pursue Matthew. I miss him and seek him out every place I go, but I had come to the conclusion I merely miss him as a dear friend and companionable presence. I was convinced my feelings for him were a product of overactive imaginations brought about by my feelings for Kirkley. I had thought 'how awkward it is to admit such a silly thing as a romantic affection for Matthew' and thought you would not approve. Now you have shone him in such a favorable light I cannot cease thinking of how good a man he is! Now you have made it seem such a sensible and natural thing for me to have fallen in love with him and are encouraging me to pursue him! Now I am in more turmoil within myself than before! Even if I am falling for him, I shan't risk ruining our friendship; it is unlikely he feels the same for me. I digress from the subject of men, I do not wish to speak of them.

We are to attend a crush tomorrow night, I look forward to it less after your account of it, I do not have a Mr Dunsworth to protect my bottom. I shall wear an extra petticoat as an additional layer of armor. Speaking of Mr Dunsworth – as you insist on loving him I have no choice but to love him too, for your sake, and hope you do not love him in vain; I am eager to hear every news of his growing fonder of you. Have you yet any hope of his loving you? Does he display any marked care or attention towards you? Do you often catch him gazing at you? Tell me all!

I cannot wait for you to join me here! Especially now I hear that Lord Miles is there and acting so strangely; how horrid Izzy! I hope he does not attack you or kidnap you! You are right in that it is most likely he is harmless, but it is still unnerving to have that man stalking you so; it makes me shudder to think of it!

Stay safe dearest!

The most love,

Your Em

Chapter 16

I have immensely distressing news, but I received your letter just as I was sat down to write you so I will briefly respond to that before returning to my original missive. With sincerity and love I commend you for your waning affections towards Mr Kirkley, and for your determination to waylay your growing reputation as a flirt. I do not commend you for your decision to ignore your feelings towards our dear Matthew. Just as you shall beg gossip of Mr Dunsworth from me, I shall continue to beg gossip of Matthew from you.

Mr Dunsworth does not gaze at me at all, that I can tell; but to catch him gazing I must also gaze at him, and I am not about to expose myself by doing so. I can think of nothing that could be considered more than the care and attention one would give a friend. There was a moment, at the crush, we danced the waltz together. He held me much tighter than necessary (though not unpleasantly so in the least!) and close enough I could have rested my head on his chest if I wished to; but it was a crush after all, there was little room for dancing; and unlike he, all my other partners bumped and bounced against other dancers like anything. I hope Matthew will be at the crush with you, I would rest easier knowing he is there to fend off the wicked fray.

Now here is the news I was first taking up the pen to write you: I will not be joining you in London Em; do not be angry with me. Nay, I do not think you could be angry with me after reading this through. It is in regards to that Lord Miles. He persists in showing up at every ball, every outing, every party we attend (accept private functions he is not invited to of course). I do not know how he knows where we are at every moment of the day, it is as if he is watching the house! I could not respectfully refuse him every time he asked me to dance, which was nearly every one, but I avoided him as best I could. His hands are always clammy and he stares so intimately into my eyes that I could not bring myself to meet his gaze even out of politeness. His conversation is focused so strongly on his own fortune, generosity, and experience one would think he believes himself the only living creature on the planet; when he does open the conversation to me it is to ask increasingly intimate questions – my favorite flower, my favorite colour, my favorite places to eat and shop and walk, where I am going after Bath, what qualities do I look for in a man, how many maids dress me in the morning, and (the most recent which had me depart from him mid-waltz) if I prefer cotton or silk undergarments! Now here is the truly terrifying piece, I will account for you as best I can. Lord Miles approached Sicily and I at the pump rooms, just after lunch, two days ago, and asked if I would be about the Sydney Gardens at all that day. I wished to avoid him of course so I politely informed him we were planning on visiting the park that day, while our true plan was to browse the shops on Pulteney Bridge before ending our day at the baths. We had a wonderful time, I purchased a number of ribbons, gloves, parasols and gowns I cannot wait to show you. Yesterday we had luncheon out-of-doors and took in a show at the Theatre Royal, and last evening attended a large crush – the particulars of who and where are unimportant. I was standing by open doors that led to the small gardens outside, Sicily had just been asked to dance and was on the arm of her partner, walking away; it is in this moment someone clutched my arm and I was all but dragged out onto the lawn. It was done so suddenly that no one immediately noticed I had vanished.

I found myself in the shadows in the presence of Lord Miles; his hands digging uncomfortably into my upper arms and his face a vision of fury. 'you!' he all but spat at me 'you lied to me!'. I begged his pardon and demanded he unhand me but his grip tightened. He then went on a tirade; I had betrayed his trust, I had treated badly and used him ill; he had waited in Sydney Gardens all day for me apparently, only to find (do not ask me how he found) that I had instead visited the shops and baths. 'How could I wound him so' he begged, and 'why would I wish to tease him'. I had no answer, I was scared dumb, like a ninny; I declare I was as white as a sheet, and trembling like anything! His person then became sweet and endearing, his hands stopped bruising me and he began stroking my paralyzed frame as if he were trying to comfort me. 'there, there, darling' he simpered, (which was frankly more terrifying than the hissing and snarling) 'do not fear me, I would never hurt you dearest' and then in complete contradiction to his previous rant 'how could I have thought you malicious, look at your sweet face, so innocent and good, you no doubt were excited to shop with your friend and merely forgot our engagement. You will not forget again, I know it...' he said more but I do not remember it, I found my voice and demanded again (quite shakily I am loath to admit) that he unhand me, and that we had no engagement, and I had no intention of going out with him anywhere, ever. He did not take it well and began to tirade again saying yet more shocking things; 'Wicked, cruel woman. Have I not done enough for you? I would die for you. Etc.' to which I replied he was being ridiculous and I didn't care for anyone to die for me. Then he grew simpering again thinking I meant I cared for him, to which I replied I did not and would never, and he PULLED OUT A KNIFE! I screamed naturally. Lord Miles pushed me against the terrace brick and covered my mouth, placing the knife against his own throat saying he could not live without me and if I did not love him then his death would be on my hands. I admit I was relieved, for I was certain he was about to murder me! Nothing came of it however for he was apprehended by the elder Mr Dunsworth. Sicily's father appeared behind him and gripped Lord Miles' wrists before he could react. Once out of danger I am ashamed to say I fainted.

I am told Eugene caught and carried me, which sounds a romantic thing in stories but allow me to disappoint you, Em love, fainting from fear and having to be picked up and carried about when limp and dead to the world is far from romantic. As a member of the female sex I am ashamed to say I have fantasized about being in a terrifying situation and carried to safety by a lover a time or two...but I wasn't even awake for the only potentially pleasant part of the whole ordeal so I wouldn't recommend any such 'romantic' adventures to anyone. I shan't be able to read silly novels anymore; I shan't be able to relate to heroines enjoying captivity after experiencing it firsthand.

I am sorry for sending you so thick a letter. To explain why I shan't join you in London: Lord Miles escaped and disappeared like a snake in the grass. He has been marked a dangerous person and is being hunted with a price on his head; but his last words to me were 'you are mine and I will find you' said very passionately as though he thought I would be thrilled about this promise, so we know he will have an eye on me. I cannot go home for Lord Miles knows where I live. My plan to visit you in London is known to him. I must go somewhere he would not think of and hide until he is caught and locked in prison. I will write you once papa is informed and a plan is made.

Matthew has been sent a letter. Stay close to him.

I miss you terribly Em!

The most love,

Your Izzy

Chapter 17

(Being Events Which Occur Between Chapter 15 and 16)

In the five day stretch of time between Miranda Riley's last letter to her sister, and Isabel's frightful responding letter, Miranda was having the most delightful time of her life. Immediately after she had sent her letter off to Isabel, she and Mrs Bertram took a pretty little curricle to visit the shops. Shortly into their ride, riding down Pall Mall, her cousin pointed at a large shop as they passed it.

"You must remind me to bring you to Harding, Howell & Co's on our way back home! Have you been? Being a department store, it does bring in some middle-class clientele...but we are not snobs" she grinned "and their selection is quite extensive and always very much in-fashion"

"I haven't been in many department stores before, but I hear that one is very grand so I shall look forward to visiting while I am here." Miranda replied cheerily. She watched people walking as they rode on until she espied, with surprise, a figure she recognized walking with a lady "Oh look! there is Mr Kirkley" then added with less enthusiasm as she noted how closely he and his companion were walking "and a...a young lady.."

Charity Bertram turned to look "Really? It is too bad we didn't notice sooner, I could have had the man stop for you! Where do you see them?" then seeing the street Miranda pointed to, she gave an incredulous chuckle. "Oh no love, I am afraid you must be mistaken, at least on the account of the lady. That is St. James's street and is known for its gentlemen's clubs and... other irreputable...establishments. No respectable lady would be seen there. With Mr Kirkley's reputation I am not surprised you saw him; men of caliber, such as my Bertram, would frequent areas of greater distinction and class."

Miranda scrunched her nose in disappointment. She was chagrined at hearing Miss Cotton's rakish description of Kirkley echoed by her Cousin; that would dispel it as a rumor, for Charity Bertram was not one for excessive gossip. Miranda concluded Kirkley was indeed a dissolute, her feelings for him had been merely fancy, and she would not seek his association longer.

Her thoughts were abandoned as they rounded a corner between Green Park and St. James's park, and Buckingham palace came into full view. Miranda's face then lit up in awe. Never had she seen a mansion of such grandeur and scale! Tall windows on every floor, great white pillars and gables expertly carved. She could only imagine what the inside of the palace would look like and, as it hid itself from view behind the trees of the lush palace garden, couldn't wait to someday take a tour within. The palace fading from view, their curricle made the short ride up Park Lane to Oxford Street, where they stepped down to the pavements of the busy shopping district and Mrs Bertram informed the driver to wait for them at Grosvenor Square.

"I have an exceptional dressmaker who owns a shop there." she explained to Miranda "Her husband is also a tailor, Mr Bertram and I go to no one else! I need to check on something I commissioned before we head home. They made the gowns mama gifted you last month!"

"Then they are exceptional in their work!" Miranda agreed as they browsed the windows of the shops.

After some purchases had been made and a Bertram servant was well stocked with packages, they walked to Grosvenor Square, stopping occasionally to speak with acquaintances they met on the way.

During a particularly lengthy conversation between her Mrs Bertram and an elderly neighbor, Miranda's eyes wandered the square, stopping in observation of a small elegant shop among the townhouses on the opposite side of the square. Her gaze lingered as she inspected what she assumed to be the shop her cousin had spoken of. Beginning to glance away, a strikingly familiar face caught her attention and snapped it back. Her breath caught in her throat as Lord Matthew Westbrook stepped smartly down the steps of the shop and strode across the square towards Hyde Park.

Blast this unending conversation! she thought in desperation as the object of her attention drew rapidly away How splendid it would have been to speak with him! And after we haven't seen each other in so long! She watched with growing irritation and disappointment until she lost sight of him and blew a great huff of vexation; to which the chattering ladies in her company either paid no heed or heard not at all.

Miranda's spirits rose marginally as the older lady took her leave a moment later and they turned toward the shop Mr Westbrook had exited a few minutes before. They entered, seeing the pleasantly chubby tailor finish placing a handsome black velvet tailcoat on a mannequin, over a dark-crimson velvet waistcoat that was decorated with fleur-de-lis embroidered in an even deeper red.

"'Allo Mrs Bertram Madam!" he greeted them with a jolly smile "Just let me finish puttin' away this here piece and I'll get the missus for ya!"

"No rush at all Mr. Chops." Mrs Bertram smiled and, pointing to the finished project he was moving to store away, noted "That is a fine ensemble you've created, I am jealous of the man who commissioned it! I don't suppose I could commission one like it for Mr Bertram?"

"Ay thank ye Madam" He chuckled "The young man just left, I believe it's for a dance or summot this evenin'. As for makin' another for your man, unfortunately not exactly. We like our creations to be unique you know, but we could tweak it a bit for ya? Maybe change the buttons to gold? The waistcoat to a soft plum or rich green?"

"Ah yes the Bradshaw social at their terrace near Kings Bridge; I assume you brought a gown appropriate for a crush Miranda?" And at Miranda's nod she turned her attention back to her tailor "That sounds lovely, as long as we keep the shape. It is a splendid cut, it would accentuate Bertram's figure quite magnificently." She said giving him a friendly wink.

As she had seen who the last gentleman to leave the shop had been, Miranda couldn't stop the image that rose in her mind of Matthew Westbrook in the dark ensemble of slightly gothic visage. She imagined it would accentuate his figure magnificently; especially considering his figure was already decidedly magnificent. With spirits now rejuvenated in full, she hoped in immense anticipation that she would see him at this evening's dance.

"You have a sharp eye Mrs Bertram!" Mr Chops laughed "I have been workin' on new styles of fit. Your husband has a physique much like this gentleman's so I can affirm the style will look positively suave on him as well!" As a stout, ambitious looking woman bustled in he extended an arm to her. "Ah, here be Mrs Chops now! Mrs Bertram here for ya love!"

Mrs Chops was just as jolly and pleasant as her significant other, but got right down to business, pulling out the gown her client had charged her with, discussing the adjustments needed (of which there were few), handing them some complimentary chocolates and sending them on their way.

They reached the Bertram's crescent terrace on Whitehall Street at roughly quarter past four and directed their packages to be sent to their rooms. They were to arrive at the Bradshaw's crush at seven or eight o'clock, they had plenty of time to prepare. Miranda and Celina, the French abigail she had brought with her to London, picked through her wardrobe thoroughly.

"Ugh! I am at a standstill Celina!" She proclaimed in exasperation, dramatically collapsing on the bed "I wish to wear the purple silk, but I feel the simpler silver gown would better suit the status of the establishment!"

"Dieu moi ma'moiselle! I wish I 'ad your troubles! But if I may be so bold, go with ze purple gown. It is to be your first crush in London, make an apparence they will not soon forget!"

"I bow to your expert advice Celina!" She hopped up and spread her arms in a gesture that said dressing may commence "bring forth the purple silk!"

Celina grinned and brought it forth, finishing up the look an hour later with strings of glittering crystals in the braids of her lady's chignon. "I believe you are ready ma'moiselle."

Turning in the mirror Miranda agreed; marveling again at the way the fabric's colour shifted between hues of deep purple and blue as she moved. Tiny crystals on the hems and bodice, blinking in the fading sunlight that seeped through the window, scattered tiny lights across the room.

She was about to exit the bedroom when she remembered something, and rushing to the vanity, rummaged through a small silver box to produce the truffle chocolate she had been given the day before.

"Here you are." She handed it to Celina with a smile "A London treat, I've had many." Then flew downstairs in a flurry of satin skirts to join her cousin at the front door, leaving a grateful and slightly bewildered Celina behind.

~~~

Miranda and her two extended family members arrived at the Bradshaw's quarter to six and separated to mingle with the other guests. She had many acquaintances there and was, therefore, quite easily introduced to whomever she wished. After an enjoyable half hour and two dances, Miranda found Grace Cotton in the crowd, greeting her greatest friend with a polite squeal of joy and a happy embrace. Miss Cotton then introduced Miranda to some of her London friends – a Mr Mastin being the only one who's name she would care to recall as he was tolerably well favored in is stature and looks; and Miranda secretly considered London to be decidedly lacking in handsome young men. She took it upon herself to gain his affections as she had no other project to occupy her time; and in her heart of hearts, she was unwilling to admit, she was angrily disappointed that she had not yet seen Matthew.

Miranda occasionally scanned the crowd throughout the third, fourth, and fifth dance, hoping to glimpse Matthew Westbrook amid the insufferable suffocating crush; but her search being fruitless, assumed regretfully he was skipping the evening entirely. A sweet elderly gentleman (who apparently knew her father) asked her for the sixth and she found him to be highly entertaining company, making her laugh often with his sarcastic humor and quick wit. Sometime during this dance, Miranda thought she saw a flash of black and red in the corner of her eye. Thinking of the outfit of Mr Westbrook's that she had seen in the shop the previous day, she glanced about to room in search of him; but being unsatisfied in her search, she returned her attention to her partner with an apology for her disregard.
~~~

As the dance neared it's end, however, she did see Mr William Kirkley, and nearly every flighty emotion she'd thought had faded in the months since he'd left Tenby flooded her once again, causing her to flush and her heart to race. Perhaps it was vexation and boredom that encouraged it, perhaps defiance against her feelings for Matthew Westbrook, but whatever the reason, every rational thought and bit of common sense within her fled.

Kirkley was dancing closely with Miss Victoria Bradshaw, and she struggled then to focus on her dance partner as both jealousy and challenge rose within her. The dance ended. Miranda expressed her sincere thanks to the older gentleman for the enjoyable dance and, agitation growing as she watched the level of camaraderie the two were displaying, she made her way towards them to greet the evening's host – and the host's partner. Kirkley noticed her, sending her a subtle wink and causing giggles of titillation to rise in her chest.

"Miss Bradshaw!" Cried she "I am glad to see you, it's been so long! This is a lively party, what a sweet little terrace your family owns!"

"Thank you Miss Riley," Miss Bradshaw returned tightly, "I hope you are enjoying yourself. Where is your friend Miss Cotton? You two are normally inseparable, she is no doubt looking for you!"

Miranda clearly caught her meaning, but would not be deterred. "Miss Cotton has many friends in London, and I could not miss out on your company Miss Bradshaw, we are friends too are we not?"

"Of course." Miss Bradshaw smiled insincerely.

"And a pleasure to see you again as well, Mr Kirkley." Miranda glanced at him; he smiled at her but, to her chagrin, still seemed more interested in her rival.

Miranda noticed Mr Mastin in the crowd watching her, an scheme formed in her mind; she gazed at him from under her lashes and, when he gave her a smile, looked away with a shy smile of her own; he began to approach much to Miranda's delight. He asked her to dance, she muttered sensually that it would be her pleasure and walked with him to the floor with a sway in her hips.

If Isabel or Matthew were observing her behavior they would be equal parts disappointed and disgusted; she tried not to care.

She allowed Mr Mastin to hold her quite close during the waltz, now-and-then meeting eyes with her Kirkley, thrilled to see his attention was now focused mainly on her.

The dance ended and Miranda was caught up in conversation with some older ladies (who had apparently known her when she was 'just the sweetest tiniest thing') when she heard a very familiar masculine voice behind her excuse himself. She began to turn to see who it was, but only glimpsed crimson velvet before a slim gloved hand appeared in front of her and she heard Kirkley's charming honey-smooth voice speak in a tone meant only for her.

"Shall we dance princess?"

Miranda's lips turned up coyly as she forced her expression not to appear as victorious as she felt. "Why Mr Kirkley, you know it would be my pleasure!" She smiled sweetly as the musicians struck up a lively tune and she was swept into his arms.

"When did you arrive?" He inquired "I did not know you were coming?"

"Why weeks ago, I would have written but you gave me no address." pouted she.

"Ah yes" he recalled after a moment "I've meant to write but I have been so very busy. I think of that night in the library often to keep me sane through the bloody monotony of every day." He smiled down at her a little, "being parted from you so long has been agony!"

"I have thought often of you as well. I've had no exciting rendezvous at all while you were gone; my romantic spirit is utterly starved!" She lamented playfully.

"Well we are together now, and you are ravishing tonight my love. The sparkles in your dress are nearly as bright as the sparkles in your eyes."

"Do be serious!" Her smile encouraged. "Not quite ravishing, to be sure!"

"I am absolutely sure, for who wouldn't find you ravishing. Especially in such a dress." He grinned.

"I don't think I can condone such flattery." She lied outrageously, then teased "For a proper gentleman would never speak of 'ravishing' so casually to a lady-friend."

"Then I am no gentleman" he smiled suggestively "and as you are no lady-friend, Princess, I shall confess that 'ravishing' is often on my mind with you."

Her mouth dropped open in an incredulous laugh at his scandalous talk; and as an unheeded visual of his implications rose in her mind, a hot blush rose to her cheeks. "Mr Kirkley! I laugh but I should not!" She giggled through her mortification, hoping no one else had heard. "Do not speak of such things in public."

"My dear Miss Ryley you are a green girl." He smirked. Seeing her pout he added "Your innocence is part of your charm, princess."

The dance ended and she took his arm as they walked off of the dance floor.

"This gathering is rather stuffy don't you think?"

"Yes! I don't understand how people bear a crush!" She affirmed, fluttering a hand near her face and wondering where in blazes she left her fan.

He leaned in towards her "Let us feed your starving romantic spirit then shall we?" then leaning closer still, whispered "Meet me in the terrace gardens in three minutes."

Her eyes widened and, placing her fingers over her mouth to hide a mischievous smile, she looked up at his expectant eyes and gave a nod. After a minute, he vanished from her side. Music rose and more dancers moved onto the floor.

Enthusiasm overtook her and less than a minute later she rushed (as surreptitiously as possible) outside into the cool night air.

Chapter 18

(A Furtherance of Events Which Occur Between Chapter 15 and 16 in Which Miranda is Very Naughty - A Warning for the More Delicate Reader...There is a Kiss Scene)

She found William Kirkley near an entrance of the hedge maze behind the long terrace of townhouses. With a furtive backwards glance, she quickly joined him and they slipped into the maze. They stood a brief moment on the wide grass paths between the tall shrubbery. Here and there lamps were stationed, throwing shadows into corners and flickering light across their faces. Kirkley gently took her hands in his. "I never thought love would come so easily or so strong." He expressed thoughtfully.

"Cupid's mind is as unpredictable as the weather." She quipped "It was a mighty arrow he struck us with it seems."

He gave a short laugh "Perhaps! Or perhaps I am lucky he found such an easy target."

"Not so easy. I am not so effortlessly caught." She pulled her gloved fingers from his grasp with a laugh.

"No?" He smirked

"I think you wish for a challenge." She assured with a grin; and picking up her skirts slightly, stepped backward away from him, beckoning him with her eyes.

"I think you are misled." He stepped towards her.

She stepped back. He rolled his eyes, smiled obligingly and walked forward. Miranda turned and with a giddy laugh began to run from him, turning deeper into the maze. She looked back as she turned the corner to see he still followed. After a few minutes of allowing him to barely touch her before running again out of his grasp, she turned to see he had disappeared.

She peeked down a few rows and, not seeing him, began to feel some fear creep into her heart that she had become lost and was alone. Panic rose in her as she turned corner after corner, minute after minute, and found not he nor the exit; but then she heard footsteps a short way down the path she was on.

With revived hope Miranda followed the light of a lantern into a cobbled garden square where a statue stood guard. The lantern behind her cast light into the far side of the small square, leaving the corners on her side dark. She smiled knowing he was near and concocted a plan to surprise him when he walked into the square as well. She quickly turned and slipped far into the deep shadows of the corner to her right, running firmly into something tall and solid.

"Ouf! Oh bother! I was planning to give you a startle but you gave me one instead!" She laughed quietly. He put a finger on her lips and she kept quiet as the figure of a man passed by a pathway leading into the square. Her heart thumped at the close call.

Once danger passed she was suddenly acutely aware of his arm around her and she realized she was pressed quite tightly against his chest - close enough to feel the embroidery on his velvet waistcoat brushing against her décolletage as she breathed with exertion - her heart thumped again for an entirely different reason. The man didn't return but they stayed in place, neither one wanting to break the embrace. After a moment her left arm, which was trapped at her side, began to feel stiff and she moved to relieve it. He loosened his grip and it seemed he was about to step away from her, much to her dismay; so she wrapped her hands around his upper arms to halt his escape with a quick and urgent hushed plea "No stay!"

She heard a sharp intake of breath but he stilled, seeming to tell her she must make the next move, so she did; stepping forward to wrap him in an embrace and lay her head against the soft fabric of his shoulder. She noticed, for the first time, he had a scent; comfortingly familiar, masculine, and utterly intoxicating! She breathed deep as his arms slipped around her, pressing her tighter against him and resting his forehead on her shoulder. She relished the feel of him; his strong arms, heart beating on her breast, soft hair caressing her cheek. She let out a happy little sigh and lifted a hand to his head where it lay beside her own, running her fingers through that silky-smooth hair. He made a strangled noise and straightened. "What..." She began. But was silenced as gloved hands touched the sides of her face and his lips pressed softly against her own.

Her initial surprise was immediately overtaken as she closed her eyes and felt a bloom of warm happy shivers grow in her chest as his lips moved on hers. This was so much better than she had dreamed, so natural and comfortable. He removed his hands from her face, leaving a tingling trail as they moved over her shoulders and down her sides to her waist. Her corset seemed to tighten and her blood began to heat. Gracious what a sweltering summer night it was, or was it just her? He deepened the kiss and at the thrill of sensation it caused in her, she concluded it was she growing hot, not the night air. A little sound escaped from her lips against his mouth. He stiffened and pulled away, still holding her. They stood breathlessly. She could make out his shape a little clearer now that her eyes had adjusted in the shadow.

"Why?" She whispered "What is it?"

"You shake me, to the core, I know not what to think." His whisper sounded strange, not his own. He lifted a hand, gently touching her cheek with his fingers, and brushing them down her neck, over her collarbone, hesitating at the swell of her breasts above her low neckline. Her breath caught and heart fluttered with a new kind of excitement she hadn't felt before. She expected she should tell him to stop.

"Is ravishing me on your mind again Kirkley?" She asked instead, startling herself with her boldness.

His hand jerked away "Wha?!.." he choked on his words, taking a step back. "I'm not....what?!?" He ran his fingers fiercely through his hair. "I...I didn't....I'm so sorry." He spun on his heel and was gone.

Miranda stood alone in the dim shadows, confusion growing to panic. At first she could not imagine what on Earth was he on about! He never had a problem trying to kiss her before, why was he sorry now?? Then she considered that perhaps it was not Kirkley she had kissed, but someone else!

No, it could not be...could it?! Dread weighed on her, she ran in the direction Kirkley had gone, finding her way out of the maze and, finally, entering the ground floor of the Bradshaw's terrace. Lips still tingling from her excursion in the garden, she checked the time (gawking as she saw nearly an hour had passed while they were outdoors) and searched the crowd for Kirkley. Where the devil was he?? How could he just leave her after such a kiss?!

The sound of someone sobbing mixed with furious whispering floated to her ears from a short, dim hall. Miranda stepped down it and peaked through the crack in the slightly open door where the sounds were coming from. She could see half of Miss Victoria Bradshaw's face, sitting crumpled in a small armchair, tears streaking her face.

"I will not allow it you good-for-nothing scoundrel!" The raspy voice shook with contained fury as the speaker paced the room, stepping into her view. Miss Bradshaw's father. "You will do the honorable thing and marry my daughter or so help me I will see you six feet in the earth!"

"Is that a threat Mr Bradshaw?" an amused voice responded. Miranda's eyes widened, her heart stopped; that voice, surely it could not be...

"You besmirch my daughter in my own home and dare to laugh at me?! It is a threat, by Jove!.." His advance towards the man out of sight was hindered by his wife clutching his arm saying low

"Stay, Mr Bradshaw, I will not have a murder in my own home!"

"I hardly besmirched her Bradshaw," the all-too-familiar voice sounded entirely bored. "We didn't get past a bit of snogging before she started mewling about it!"

"Not true and you know it, William Kirkley!" choked out the young Miss Bradshaw, "you lifted my skirts, you t-tried to touch me!"

"But I didn't now did I? Daddy came and saved you before anything naughty happened, as though you weren't begging for it in the first place."

"I wa-wasn't begging f-for..!" Miss Bradshaw's crying overtook her words. Miranda's heart sunk, she could listen no more, she wished to leave this horrid crush. As Miranda turned away she did not see young Miss Bradshaw's eyes land on her through the crack and widen in terror.

Fleeing the secret scene, Miranda spotted Grace Cotton near the front hall talking and laughing with someone out of her view. As she drew closer she saw it was cousin Edwin Lawrence, and someone who looked suspiciously like Matthew Westbrook. She hurried forward with renewed purpose, forgetting about Kirkley (but not quite forgetting about the kiss or the argument she had witnessed). Alas, Edwin and Matthew turned and took their leave before she could break through the crush to reach them. Desperate for comfort, for a piece of home, she pushed past Miss Cotton with a brief, "Forgive me Grace, love." before hurrying out the door after Matthew. Her heart sunk yet further as she stepped onto the dark streets to see him turn his horse around a corner and out of sight.

She'd missed him. She blinked back hot tears. Curse the hedge maze! Curse Mr Kirkley! Curse bloody London! Miranda wished for home, beloved Tenby Hall.

~~~

Miranda Riley reluctantly tossed and turned in her bed that night, her mind a tumult of thought. She despised herself. She had allowed herself to be foolishly played with by a man of shockingly bad character; a mouse flirting with a fox. She'd willingly given in to his false flattery, thrown herself into his wicked schemes, believed herself to be in love, believed herself to be in control! She'd felt fancy; no, thrill – the thrill of secrecy, flirtation, and (she blushed in mortification) lust.

Poor, poor Miss Bradshaw. The rat of a man! Thought she, He must have grown bored with my playful game of catch-me-if-you-can and left me in the maze in search of easier prey! She grimaced at the memory of her actions in hindsight, running playfully and trustingly from no one, as Kirkley grew bored and sought out Miss Bradshaw.

But then, she felt sick, I kissed a stranger. Judging by their apology they were somewhat of a gentleman; hopefully they would tell no one. She could not think who it could be, and the more she thought of the possibilities she realized ashamedly that there was more than one man who might
~~~

believe she would follow him for a tryst! Not that she was a determined flirt, but there were three she finally settled on as suspects, which was a good two or three more than there should be: Mr Craig, a Mr Weller, and the young Mr Mastin.

She struggled to recall anything about the man she had kissed. Velvet waistcoat, taller than her by a head, short hair – but long enough to comfortably run fingers through...she sighed...then lightly smacked her own cheek in fury at herself. Stop dreaming of a first kiss that you willingly gave to a stranger you hussy! That ruled out Mr Craig as his hair was nearly shoulder-length, and Mr Weller wasn't more than inch taller than her at most (though she and Izzy were taller than the average girl). She could not recall if Mr Mastin had worn velvet but he was the right height with shorter hair, she would have to confront him alone as soon as she could and beg his forgiveness and confidence.

One of the greatest sorrows of the evening was that she had, once again, failed to speak to her dear Matthew; oh, how she wished to see him, she desperately needed something of the comforts of home, and who in London could give it but he!

Chapter 19

(A Furtherance of Events Which Occur Between Chapter 15 and 16)

A polite rapping on her chamber door at the ungodly hour of nine woke her the next morning, and she rose sorely moaning when it would not cease.

"A visitor for ye Miss." she was told. "A young lady in a bad way. She asks if she may see ye in your rooms when you're ready." Alarmed, Miranda allowed it, and had herself dressed as quickly as she could. The maid brought the girl when instructed and, to her surprise, Miranda found the door closed behind Miss Victoria Bradshaw.

"Miss Bradshaw....what...?" She nearly stammered in shock at the young woman who stood before her, pale, eyes bloodshot and swollen.

"Do forgive me Miss Riley, but if I am not mistaken, you witnessed..som ething..last night."

Miranda, cheeks pink with shame, gestured for the girl to take a seat in one of the armchairs that sat in her room. "I did eavesdrop, it was very wrong of me, but if you have come to ask me not to gossip on the matter then allow me to put your fears to rest.."

"I confess that was partly my purpose in coming."

"I am not one to spread rumors."

"I did not think you were, but you would be full within your right to spread the truth."

"Well I reiterate: you may have confidence in my promise of silence Miss Bradshaw." She settled into the remaining armchair. "What was the other part of your purpose in coming?"

"I wished to warn you away from him." she muttered. "I know you fancied him as I did."

"Ah, that is admirable of you. The little I witnessed last night warned me well enough; any shallow feelings I may have had for him are waning rapidly."

Miss Bradshaw looked as though she might begin to cry once more.

"Forgive me as it's not my place, but, he did not ruin you?.."

"No. I would not let him..." her voice cracked and chin trembled. "You may be disappointed by Mr Kirkley, Miss Riley, but this is my third season, I have no prospects, and no money.."

"But your parents make nearly eight-thousand a year!" Miranda interrupted.

"Oh, they aren't my real parents, they are my aunt and uncle. My parents died and their fortune fell on my younger brother. I have no dowry." Miranda understood then, nothing more need be said. With no dowry, no gentleman would attach themselves to her except he love her unconditionally – which was unlikely knowing how rare such love was. Miss Bradshaw must marry for money, if she could, or else she would be forced to live as a spinster or a governess. Miranda pitied the girl who sat across from her, she made the resolution to be compassionate and kind to her from now on, sorry she had not been before.

~~~

Not ten minutes after Miss Bradshaw left was Miranda's door rapped upon once more, much to her great astonishment.

"Another visitor for ye Miss." she was informed.

This time Miss Cotton was let in, apologizing profusely for her unannounced appearance so early in the day. "But look, perhaps I needn't worry now I see you are already up and dressed.."

"No, you needn't worry about a thing; see, you aren't the first to surprise me with a visit this morn. It appears my bedchamber is quite 'the place to be' today."

"Oh! Who.."

"The lady begged my confidence so I cannot say. Pray tell what urgent matter it is that has brought you to me in such haste."

"I hope this does not make you think badly of me.." Miss Cotton set herself on the edge of the bed with a wriggle and crossed her ankles. "I hope it is not to intrusive or forward but I feel I must warn you – as a friend who loves you - about Mr Kirkley."

"Lord have mercy, there is another."

"I dare say there is an army, if you are speaking of Mr Kirkley's conquests."

"You are not ruined?"

"I did not suffer ruination, no; only a broken heart once I learned of how ill he'd used other members of the female sex, and had to break it off before the same happened to me. I don't know why he chased me so long or why
~~~

he insisted on continuing our courtship when I said I would not, for I never allowed him to kiss me or even hold me. I can see how other women were so easily wooed by him, he always seemed so very sincere and sure, so down-to-earth."

"The Kirkley Miss Bradshaw and I know is far from down-to-earth." Miranda commented dryly, then chuckled. "Maybe he almost had real feelings for you..."

"I don't know..." Miss Cotton's fingers fidgeted; her pretty features downcast. "If he did have hopes for me, they didn't take long to heal after I disappointed them."

~~~

Miranda saw Kirkley at a ball that night, but did not deign to speak to him – which didn't seem to injure him in the least. After he greeted her and found himself facing the flat side of her fan, he forgot she existed.

~~~

While Isabel was in Bath experiencing The Frightening Encounter, Miranda was, in the meanwhile, watching an opera in a comfortable box and trying to catch the eye of Mr Mastin who sat in a box opposite.

The shimmering blue peacock of a woman below hit an unearthly note and Mr Mastin' eyes slid to hers, and in recognizing her, focused on her. Success. Miranda Riley smiled sincerely and was rewarded with a smile in return. During intermission she sought him out and, to her satisfaction, he found her.

"How are you enjoying Acis and Galatea?"

"Galatea sings with great passion."

"And we have not yet reached the scenes that require it."

"You have seen it before?"

"Of course! I love an opera, there is such feeling in the singers and script, it moves the soul!"

A man who truly loved the arts and not the singer's bosom?! Miranda was impressed. "It is a wonderful story, despite being a tragedy."

"Ah, but tragedy makes it more real, more relatable."

"Does Acis and Galatea remind you of your own tragedies then? A giant murdered your lover?" grinned she. "Will you also immortalize said lover in stone?"

He laughed. "You mock me. I shan't take offence; you do not appreciate the arts."

"P'shaw." exclaimed she. "I shall be the better man and meet your insult with a compliment. That is a fine blue velvet. Velvet is not a common fabric for waistcoats. Were you wearing it at Bradshaw's the other night as well?"

"I may have been," answered he with a laugh. "I don't fully recall, but it is a favorite of mine."

"You wear it well sir." she smiled, thinking Mr Mastin absolutely must be the man from the garden. "I have a matter I would like to speak with you on. Would you meet with me tomorrow in Hyde park?"

"I would. I am free around two o'clock."

"I will meet you there with my cousin then, thank you. I must return to my box, enjoy the rest of the show Sir."

"You as well Miss, I look forward to the morrow." He tipped his hat with a smile, she returned to her box. They exchanged glances throughout the remainder of the opera; raised eyebrows at particularly high notes, and amused looks during humorous bits and slip-ups. Acis was dramatically killed and Miranda caught glanced at Mr Mastin; he dabbed his eyes, she rolled hers, he chuckled. Miranda Riley considered the evening overall delightful.

~~~

Two o'clock in Hyde Park, Miranda and Mrs Bertram sat on a bench together in lively conversation. Mr Mastin appeared and approached, bowing to the ladies in greeting. The ladies rose and Miss Riley took his offered arm. They walked, with Mrs Bertram a polite distance behind.

After the natural pleasantries two friendly acquaintances might share on a casual stroll at the end of summer, Mr Mastin recalled his companion had a purpose in meeting with him today, and begged it of her. She removed her arm from his and clutched her hands together.

"Well, I'm not quite sure how to begin. I wanted to ask you...at the Bradshaw crush...did you happen to follow me.." she noticed he had become quite red and disquieted, smiling nervously.

"Ooh.." murmured she. He most definitely was the one who had kissed her that night.

"Yes, I was watching your exchanges with him. I saw you were very close. I saw Kirkley leave, and – I must admit I don't like the man in the least – you after him so, yes, I followed; but you must understand I was thinking only of your safety! I had no intention of.."

"I know Mr Mastin, I know you are a gentleman and I thank you for your concern. Kirkley is not a good man and I am ashamed I allowed him so close to my person. I will speak of that night no longer except to say I am glad it was you! We can remain friends?"
~~~

"Of course, Miss Riley!" He said with alarm. "Why ever would we not be?? Although.." he continued abashedly "..I would prefer to be more one day; if you would allow me to court you."

Miranda was startled. "Why Mr Mastin! I did not think you would...you do not think ill of me after...?"

"No, Miss Riley, why on earth would I think ill of you?? No, you did nothing wrong."

Miranda Riley was relieved and flattered. She blushed prettily. "Well, I suppose it would make sense...under the circumstances.."

He raised his eyebrows in amusement after a moment. "Is that meant to be a consent?" She blushed harder. "Yes..you may court me, Mr Mastin."

He smiled and offered her his arm once more, she took it happily. Mrs Bertram watched in satisfaction.

~~~

The following morning Miranda received a letter from Isabel that distressed her beyond measure. Miranda would not leave her room for fear (and because her eyes were embarrassingly red from crying).

Mr Mastin came calling that afternoon but was told there was a family emergency and, respectfully, it was not an ideal time to visit. He nodded a greeting to the arriving Matthew Westbrook on his way out.

At hearing who the second visitor was, Miranda nearly dove down the stairs in her rush see him. She threw herself into his arm with enthusiasm, tears falling anew. Matthew consoled and quieted her, holding her tight in his arms, murmuring words of comfort and telling her Izzy was safe and all would be well.
~~~

"Poor, poor Izzy!" she lamented with a sniffle, now sitting comfortably in the parlor with her cousins and Westbrook. "How could this happen to her! She is so good, and sensible, and would never flirt or lead a man to believe she cared for him more than she did! She does not deserve it! If it happened to anyone it should have happened to me!"

"Certainly not!" Matthew exploded, causing her to jump. "Don't say such things! It shouldn't happen at all! Least of all to you!" He calmed himself, laying a tender hand on her arm. "Lord Miles is a mentally unstable leech of a man. There is no one at fault for his actions but he."

"Poor Izzy." sighed she again. "To be stalked so; to have to be hidden away lest she is taken captive! It is like something out of a story, it cannot be real!"

"We can't despair, we must pray for Izzy and wait for word from your father on what is to be our next move." Charity Bertram reasoned.

"She cannot remain in London, surely; not with the possibility of Lord Miles coming here." Mr Bertram spoke then.

"Oooh! Imagine if he mistook me for Isabel..!" this was gasped by a horror-stricken Miranda.

Matthew Westbrook's face took on a strained expression, hand tightening a little on her arm. "You cannot stay in London. I must take you home." Miranda had no inclination to argue.

They did not have to wait long before a letter from Lord Riley arrived instructing Westbrook to bring his daughter home to Tenby post-haste; and post-haste they came. Once home, Miranda sent a brief letter to Mr Mastin informing him that she had returned home emergently and was terribly sorry she had not been able to say goodbye; and that, should he wish to write her, she would look forward to his letter.

She wished she could write her sister, but no one could tell her where Izzy was.

Chapter 20

Lord Riley and Mr Dunsworth Sr sent express letters to each other via Lord Riley's private messenger. Lord Riley and Miranda were sick with worry, as was Mr Wesbrook who returned to Tenby hall as often as he could, bringing news, distraction, and whatever support and comfort his person could extend. Lady Isabel Riley was confined to her room in Bath under careful watch lest Lord Miles attempt to abscond with her again. Sicily and Eugene did not abandon their friend, they spent the three days following The Frightening Encounter – as they called it – in her room playing games, chatting, and trying to entertain themselves in general. The third day they were informed of Lord Riley and Mr Dunsworth's plan. Isabel would be sent to the Dunsworth's home two days ahead of them, she would exit the building through the servants' quarters and step immediately into a carriage which would take her straight to Blackstone Abbey – the Dunsworth's home in Southamptons. Eugene Dunsworth would be riding with her for her safety. The word would be spread Isabel was in London, and Matthew was to remove Miranda from London as soon as was possible.

Isabel and Mr Dunsworth stood inside the servants' entrance, ready to depart. She held a carpetbag with two changes of clothes only. Miss

Dunsworth held her friend tearily, Isabel petted Miss Dunsworth's short hair consolingly.

"I will come to no harm, Sicily, your brother is with me to ensure that. I am forever in your family's debt for saving me – twice over – I am so sorry to be halting your lovely vacation and forcing myself into your home. I should be the one crying, for am sorry and ashamed I have become a nuisance to your wonderful family."

"Nay!" Miss Dunsworth exclaimed "You are expected to cry, but for fear, not because of shame! How dare you consider yourself a nuisance! We are happy to aid you, and more than happy to have you in our home! Eugene, assure her!"

"Oh no, please don't feel obli.."

"I assure you," Mr Dunsworth obliged, interrupting Isabel, "the only thing that could make us happier is if you were returning home with us of your own free will."

"Oh no! I am...I wish to go!"

"Yes, but would that it were under more pleasant circumstances; circumstances that allowed you the choice not to."

"He means he is sorry for The Frightening Encounter that led to us having to pack you off in secret." Sicily comforted "Not that he thinks you do not wish to visit Thornhill."

Mr Dunsworth looked away and acted as though it was high time they were on their way.

"We really must be off Sicily," Isabel urged "I will see you in a short few days." Miss Dunsworth teared up again, and with a kiss for Isabel's cheek waved her off.

The dark carriage trundled through town and into the country. There was silence for many, many minutes before Isabel spoke to the man in the opposite corner. "It is not what you meant is it."

"Of what do you speak?" he regarded her.

"You said: you wished I had the choice not to come to Thornhill; and your sister claimed you meant you were sorry I experienced The Frightening Encounter, not sorry I had no choice but to come."

"I am sorry for your experience, it is horrifying and I wouldn't wish it on any woman."

"Yes, but you believe if Lord Miles had never existed, I would never wish to visit Blackstone, and are sorry I have to come at all."

"I am not sorry you have to come, you are a friend of my family, why would I be sorry to host a friend."

Isabel sighed with exasperation. "Stop avoiding the point. I believe you are sorry for my sake because you think I would not choose to visit Blackstone, were I invited."

He looked out the window and did not deny it.

"I am thrilled to visit Southamptons and join you and your family in Blackstone. Why do you think I would be unhappy there? Do you think me prejudiced? Have I offended you somehow?" asked she sincerely.

He inhaled and exhaled a great breath, and looked at her "You have not offended me Miss Riley, I do not think you could. I think you good, and kind; but you are a Lady, a debutante, used to wealth and lavishness and all manner of fine things. If I think you prejudiced I do not think it with judgement or fault. No, I don't believe you will be content or 'happy' residing in a small abbey for any extended period of time; you will become bored, and you will find it difficult living without luxury or staff in every room."

Isabel's shoulders slumped. "I have offended you." she determined sadly "You do not think well of me."

He watched her a moment as she tugged at her shawl's fringe, looking very melancholy indeed. "I think very well of you Miss Riley."

Her eyes met with his, tentatively. A smile twitched on her lips as she entwined her fingers and looked down at her hands. "I am relieved. I hope I can prove to you that I am capable of being more than a debutant. I think I am not so depthless as to require luxury."

He offered her a small smile. "You have depth enough to appreciate roman history and a quiet evening by a fire, perhaps the Abbey may extend enough charm to endear you to it."

"I dare say anyone would prefer an abbey over a manor, if that were not so there would be far less novels set in them." they chuckled over this together.

After many hours the rolling of the carriage lulled Isabel to sleep, her head bumping lightly against the cushioned sides. The horses took a corner sharply and she began to tip over, nearly falling into the aisle. Eugene Dunsworth caught her quickly and gently lowered her so she lay on the carriage seat with her head resting on her carpet bag. Dunsworth watched her for a moment, breathed a short laugh, then gazed outside. Soon after, he too slept. Isabel was woken by his voice calling her name.

"What is it?" slurred she, drunk on sleep.

"We arrive shortly."

It was black outside, the crescent moon dim and stars clouded over. The night was cool and the carriage retained little warmth. "Ouf." Isabel shuddered against the cold as she rubbed her drowsy eyes.

Dunsworth shrugged off his travelling cloak and handed it to her. "It will not be twenty minutes and we will be enjoying a warm fire at Blackstone."

She sent him a grateful smile, taking his cloak and using it as a blanket, clutching it under her chin. "It is unfortunate it is night; I would have liked to first see it in daylight."

"You will see it on the morn."

"That is a long time to suffer anticipation." she laughed lightly.

"It is a hut compared to Tenby; your anticipation will find little reward."

"Mr Dunsworth, for shame; I am beginning to think you more prejudiced than I!"

"And how have you come to that conclusion?!" He did not seem offended.

"Do you think so little of Blackstone? do you have no pride in it? Either you are displeased with it because you do not think it good enough for you, or you are ashamed of it because to do not think it good enough for society."

"If it were either it would be the latter. It is not myself nor society that concerns me; and I have great pride in Blackstone."

"Then I do not understand why you do not sing its praises." Dunsworth said nothing. "I am convinced it is the handsomest house in all of Southamptons and I shan't be disappointed." promised she decidedly.

"It is a very 'handsome' house, as you say; but it is still only a small abbey, no matter how handsome, and a palace will always be preferred."

"I do not know why you insist on being so contemptuous." She muttered angrily under her breath, looking out to the passing trees.

"I am not contemptuous; I merely do not set my sights higher than what I have a right to." Explained he, frustration tinging his voice, irritating her further.

"What??" She faced him. "What do you speak of?" Annoyance caused her to demand. "It does not sound as though you speak of houses any longer, what is it you believe you do not have a right to?"

He looked suddenly unsure of how to respond, something akin to panic in his eyes. He could not face her, and turned to focus out the carriage window, choosing to change the subject completely. "Tomorrow I must visit a family by the name of Wescott, you may come with me if you do not wish to remain at Blackstone alone."

"I am not opposed to making new acquaintances; I will come, thank you." she agreed after a short silence. "They are good friends of your family then?"

"Not great friends. I.." there was a painfully long stretch of silence wherein he clenched and unclenched his jaw and his hands tightened into fists. Isabel stared, a little alarmed, a little concerned. He looked her in the eyes. "I am courting their daughter, Miss Amie Wescott..." Isabel's face drained of colour. "It would cause offence if I did not visit her first thing." Finished he, gazing out the window once more.

"Naturally." she replied in weak agreement. There was no conversation the short remainder of the journey. Isabel felt as though she might cast up her accounts and refrained from looking at Mr Dunsworth lest she gain a silly inclination to cry. Why had she agreed to join him tomorrow! She would fabricate an excuse and would not go.

Chapter 21

I t took Isabel Riley a moment to recall where she was the next morning. She gazed about the small bedchamber she had awoken in and shivered as it was a little cool. The furniture and general décor were high quality and quite in season, though not in as much abundance as her own room. A maid lighting a small hearth was what had woken her. "Excuse me, Girl," she asked, "what time is it?"

"Quarter to eleven, Miss."

Isabel thought it odd the maid would be just lighting a fire now, it should be lit much earlier to warm the room before the lady woke. Dunsworth's voice in her mind then spoke I don't believe you will be content residing in a small abbey; you will find it difficult living without luxury, or staff in every room. Isabel, stiff-necked and tenacious, would not allow his prediction to become true; she threw off her warm quilt, forcing herself not to balk at there being no rug between her bare feet and the chilly floor-boards.

"I unpacked yer bag, Miss. Yer clothes are in tha' there closet. I was instruct-ed to help you dress." the scrawny little maid gave a small curtsy. "Will ye be wanting the blue or the lavender today?"

Isabel missed her three pretty French and Italian abigails from home, this girl did not look like she would be able to tie a proper corset. You do not need three lady's maids to dress you, you spoiled prissy she scolded herself. She smiled kindly. "The blue pinstripe will do, thank you."

"Do ye want the corset tight as what'av ye or do you prefer it loost?"

Isabel stared at the girl. "Why would I want a loose corset??"

The girl shrugged, looking a mite spanked. "I dunno Miss, tha's how the Miss Dunsworths likes it. S'pose it's more comfortable."

Feeling rebellious, Isabel grinned, "I'll have it however she does then." It wasn't as though she had anyone to impress in any case.

She wandered downstairs, adjusting a thick shawl about her shoulders, surveying the rest of the house. It was much, much smaller than Tenby, but not uncomfortably so. It was very stylish and bright – for an abbey – and larger than she had admittedly imagined (though Eugene Dunsworth could be blamed for her low expectations). Four floors and three towers, many spacious rooms, a well-tended courtyard and garden, and a large woodland to explore which covered most of the estate. It could not be considered insufficient, far less 'poor'. Isabel was well pleased. She had glimpsed the outdoors from through windows, now she ventured out into it. She walked to the far end of the courtyard to turn and view the abbey, tucked into the woods, as she had been unable to upon arriving last night. The word she decided fit it best was enchanting. The dark weathered brick, hugged – nay, overwhelmed – by ivy, stood before her proud; yet also humbled by time. Dunsworth stepped around a corner and, seeing her, approached.

"How was your night?"

"Very comfortable, thank you. Where have you been this morning?"

"The stables; there is a new colt old enough to begin breaking, I have been letting him get used to me."

"You are a lover of horses?"

"Sicily claims I am wild for them. I would not go so far, but I admire and respect them a great deal. What is it makes you stand out here so still and contemplative?"

She turned toward him slightly with a smile "It is Blackstone, I am inspired by her. She radiates a character almost human."

"Ah." His lips twitched and eyes filled with amusement, following her gaze to his home. "Pray tell: what is it she inspires in you, and what do you suppose her character to be?"

"She inspires wonder and...if beauty were a feeling...I suppose." She obliged. "Her character would be poised, charming, and esoteric; she would have a vague and mysterious story the like of which everyone would wish to hear; yet she would tell only one."

"And who is this 'one' she would tell her story to?"

"The one she still waits for." Isabel smiled, "She looks like she's been waiting quite some time." He chuckled then. "Yes, father has been meaning to freshen up Blackstone's exterior for some time now. It will be a tedious job to remove so much vine, and repair the brick. I don't think he will ever get around to it."

"But he would not do it, surely he would hire men for the task."

"Yes, obviously; however, working men require wages. Not that we couldn't afford it, but my father is too cautious with his money. I cannot even convince him to invest it."

"Caution is not a great fault...Say, when are you to visit your Miss Wescott? It is nigh on two!"

"I suppose I must be on my way." conceded he irritably, "Will you come or shall you remain?"

"I feel it would be more appropriate for you to visit without me this afternoon. I can meet them another day."

He nodded, then departed alone.

~~~

Three days Isabel roamed the halls and acres of Blackstone; and with joy and relief on the third, welcomed home Mr and Mrs Dunsworth and their daughter.

"You know," Isabel commented to Sicily Dunsworth as they walked – arms interlinked – up to the front door, "I have done some exploring since I arrived and have found your little trout pond; it is not nearly as little as I imagined, and there is a brook running through it so it is very fresh..you did not do it justice when you spoke of it at Tenby."

"Ah, well, it isn't a murky puddle to be sure; but one still smells somewhat fishy after a swim in it."

"I must prove that claim as soon as weather permits."

Behind them someone scoffed good-naturedly. "As if having my sister stinking up the house wasn't enough."

"Oh you! It isn't nearly so bad!" She spun and swatted at him. "Don't insult our guest Eugene!"

"I wouldn't dare." smirked he, dodging, and strode past them poised and unruffled.
~~~

"What an odd creature my brother is." Sicily huffed.

"His character is so different in the comfort of his own home, I never could have imagined it." Isabel smiled, watching him bound up the stairs to the second floor.

"Yes! He acts so proper and decent when in public, one would never imagine he were such a nuisance." Sicily laughed as the two girls turned into the front parlor.

"Nay! He is playful, not a nuisance!"

"You do not have to live with him! If you did, the 'playfulness' would soon become a nuisance."

"You are like my sister. Matthew Westbrook – who is like a brother to us – he teases her mercilessly because her reactions are more entertaining than mine. She is irritated by him, I am more inclined to tease him in return."

Miss Dunsworth grinned. "You are right, he is not malicious, I should not so easily take offense; but more than that, I am flattered you compare me to a twin sister."

"You are very quickly becoming a sister to me. I am so glad I am to hide at Blackstone, I feel as safe and contented here with you and your family as I would my own."

"Cease your flattery," Demanded Sicily, her bright eyes growing watery. "Look, you cause me to leak!" she rubbed the tear away.

"Bless me, very well, no more compliments." Was the laughing response.

"Tell me," Sicily spoke in hushed tones, abruptly standing and shutting the parlor door. "Has Eugene yet visited a Miss Wescott since he arrived home??"

"He has, yes." Isabel tried to maintain her smile. "Two days ago I believe.. .yes, the day after we arrived."

"Just the once?"

"Yes..."

"Oh good. If a man really loved a woman would you not expect him to wish to see her every day, if not more often?"

Isabel was confused. "I imagine it depends on the man."

"Well we are speaking of Eugene, obviously."

"You know him better than I!"

"I do not think he really loves her." Miss Dunsworth stated "Have you yet met Miss Wescott?"

"I have not."

"I do not like her. She has not a penny to her name and I am sure she cares for my brother's money more than the man himself."

"You cannot assume such a thing just because she is poor."

"I don't base assumptions on such things Miss Riley, it is her manner that does not recommend her."

"But Mr Dunsworth is a sensible man, surely he would not be easily deceived."

"We can hope. Mama will invite them for dinner soon and you shall have the occasion to form your own opinion."

~~~
~~~

Isabel's opinion was quickly formed upon meeting the Wescotts, and she was quite in agreement with Miss Dunsworth. Mr and Mrs Wescott were pleasant enough, there was nothing very interesting or remarkable about them. Mr Westcott was moderately serious in expression and conversation, his wife fairly expressive in contrast. Miss Amie Wescott, however, was too pleasant. Everything little thing about Blackstone and the Dunsworths was to be complimented, every conversation to be entered, every person to be intimately known.

She descended on Isabel Riley immediately, wishing to know all her family and acquaintances – did Isabel have brothers, how thrilling it must be to have a twin sister, how many did they dine with; the details of Tenby hall – if it was very large, how many gardens, if it was decorated in a French or Greek style (it was neither); of Miss Riley's own interests – did she like balls and wouldn't it be lovely to have a dance while she was here, if all her gowns were as lovely as the one she now wore, did she love London and Bath (begging descriptions of each).

The second time it was expressed how unfortunate it was the Miss Riley's were not blessed with a brother Isabel countered that they had a very close friendship with a one Mr Westbrook who was every bit like a brother to them, therefore, she did not feel she was unfortunate in the least. Miss Wescott then demanded the attention of Eugene Dunsworth away from his conversation with the other two men so she may ask him if he knew Isabel's Mr Westbrook well. It was at this moment Isabel Riley concluded Miss Amie Wescott would not do for Mr Eugene Dunsworth. She looked to Miss Dunsworth who watched her friend with a question in her eyes; Isabel shook her head ever so slightly, Miss Dunsworth was satisfied.

Chapter 22

A month passed. Lord Miles still remained undetected and, as a consequence, Isabel Riley remained confined in hiding.She did not mind. She grew ever closer to Sicily Dunsworth, her longing for Tenby and her Em eased by baths in Blackstone's trout pond with Sicily, reading and dancing together by the hearth as the weather grew cooler, secretly relishing the moments she enjoyed in Mr Dunsworth's company – growing unfortunately more in love with him and his home the longer she lingered there.

It pained and quieted her whenever in the presence of Miss Wescott, mainly because when alone with Miss Riley the woman would not cease in her exclamations of Dunsworth's loyalty and care towards her and how fine and handsome he was and how she was sure he must speak to her father soon. Isabel was in agony these hours and could not bring herself to speak.

They sat in the parlor of Blackstone one afternoon, Eugene, Miss Dunsworth, Isabel, and Miss Wescott, speaking of faraway places.

"You are so lucky to have seen so much of the world Miss Riley!"

"I have hardly seen the world Miss Wescott, I have not been outside of England.."

"Oh what I wouldn't give to travel! One day I will experience all the diversions London, Bath, Paris, and Rome can offer!"

"Those are expensive and time-consuming trips, I wonder at how you will achieve this goal."

"You would crush my dreams Miss Riley," the girl laughed "but I will not be disheartened. I am determined. Fortune favors those who seek it."

"Yes, and you seek it boldly. You will succeed." Isabel smiled sweetly (though a little insincerely).

Miss Wescott nodded in self-satisfaction. "And until I am able to travel all of England in fine gowns and phaetons, I must content myself with traveling to the seaside. Before you left for Salisbury you promised me there would be an excursion to the seaside Mr Dunsworth, do you recall? It must be done before the really cold weather sets in."

"Oh did you promise a seaside excursion Mr Dunsworth? How lovely! You will honor the promise? I have not yet been to the seaside since arriving."

"Oh, he will honor it, Miss Riley; Mr Dunsworth is the most honorable man I know!" Miss Wescott assured before he could respond. She continued, gazing at him rather pointedly, "He would never raise hopes or expectations in anyone if he did not think he would follow through."

Mr Dunsworth mostly contained his irritation, Miss Wescott's meaning a little too clear to all. "You will get your seaside excursion." He allowed stoically from where he stood by the window. "We will set out next week, Saturday. There, I have followed through on my promise, are you satisfied Miss Wescott?"

Amie Wescott's desire was indeed suffonsified.

~~~
~~~

Next week, Saturday, was a pleasantly mild day, though a little gray. Gulls called and dove at brackish waters that roughened the rocky shore, the playful breeze tickling their feathers lifting them far over the heads of the eight visitors wandering below. Isabel Riley stood watching the sea with Miss Wescott and Dunsworth – who customarily remained silent when with these two girls together.

"I do so love the sea." Isabel breathed, entranced by the white tips of passionate waves that stretched out of sight. She breathed deep the salty-sweet air.

"It is pretty, but it smells so.." sighed Miss Wescott.

"It is pretty," Isabel smiled happily at the young woman beside her. "It's beautiful, so powerful and free, don't you think?"

Miss Wescott glanced at Isabel, thinking her odd. "I suppose."

"You've been to the sea before Miss Wescott?"

"Yes, once or twice, but I'm beginning to wonder why I wished to return." was the response, lightened by a laugh.

"It is not what you remembered?" Isabel smiled.

"It's rather boring now I'm here." laughed she as though she expected Miss Riley to agree.

"At least it is a change in scenery, the air is clean and the breeze is refreshing."

"Well I'm glad someone finds it refreshing. It is too chilly so close to the water, I wish there was less wind." complained Miss Wescott, her simpering, cheerful manner fading.

"You may have my shawl if you like, it is a little more substantial than yours." Offered Isabel.

"Oh la, I think not, Miss Riley, it would clash horridly with my dress." Miss Wescott declined as if that were an obvious thing.

"You are to catch your death of a cold in want of preserving a fashionable ensemble??" Isabel was amazed.

"La! It is not all that cold Miss Riley, how dramatic you are! The wind merely needs calm a little."

Isabel struggled to hide her incredulity. "I certainly hope you do not depend upon it." Dunsworth's lips twitched, his gaze remained on the horizon.

"I dislike wind." Miss Wescott sighed. "My hair will be irreparable after today, and my ribbons are coming undone I'm sure."

"There, there Miss Wescott, let us be sensible." Miss Riley consoled. "Your hair will be easily repaired, for there is hardly one strand out of place that I can observe; and your ribbons are only fluttering slightly – not nearly enough to come undone."

Miss Wescott fussed with her curls and seemed pleased. Dunsworth hid his amusement. Isabel thought she might, for a moment, have begun disrespecting him a little for his choice in a life partner; but then she gave him the benefit of the doubt, for perhaps he had few options in that respect, and he had not yet offered for her so there was hope he might yet redeem himself.

"Bless me," Miss Wescott observed nasally, "Miss Dunsworth has removed her shoes and stockings, do not tell me she is going to wade.."

"I believe she is! What a splendid idea!" Isabel grinned. "I think I shall join her."

"You cannot be serious!" Miss Wescott gaped. "How raffish!"

"Miss Wescott what a prude you are." Isabel commented, exasperated. "Will you come Mr Dunsworth? I know you will have no qualms with wading."

With a glance at the expectant Miss Wescott he replied, "I will remain, Miss Riley, thank you."

"Ah, yes." Isabel could not conceal the disappointment behind her jest. "Your reputation must be maintained and Miss Wescott must be entertained."

Miss Wescott was affronted and Dunsworth's expression bordered on a frown. Swallowing her guilt, Isabel hurried to join Miss Dunsworth. Peeking at the two she left behind as she unbuttoned her shoes, she found them talking with heads inclined closely towards each other; Miss Wescott glanced towards her and Isabel snapped her face away.

"You are joining me!" Miss Dunsworth noted gleefully as her mother tut-tutted and told them they should not be exposing themselves in such a manner in front of Miss Wescott, to which Sicily replied Miss Wescott best get used to it if she planned on espousing herself with Eugene in the future. Walking together through the frothy waves lapping the shore, Isabel asked Sicily if she'd ever spoken to her brother about Miss Wescott – specifically, what it was he saw in her – and what (this question she kept secretly to herself) was so appealing in Miss Wescott that Isabel herself was lacking.

"My brother rarely allows me a glimpse into the inner workings of his mind..." Miss Dunsworth slid her bonnet off her head, her boyishly short hair whiffling in the breeze. "as a consequence, I have little to share on the subject. I suspect he knows she needs his money more than she needs him, but then, that's the way of the world is it not?" a wry smile flickered on her face. "Who ever marries for love? The richer one is, the higher one set one's sights." "Yes. I suppose you would think that." Isabel agreed starchily. "My sister and I are lucky our papa wishes us to marry for love. He always told us he was blessed he and Mama enjoyed such a happy marriage - though he had but two years with her - and that he would not see us unhappy were it with the richest man in the world."

"I did not mean to offend.."

Isabel smiled sheepishly. "..and I did not mean to snap. I know you do not think me a fortune-chaser." She breath a short sigh, looked briefly backwards to where Dunsworth and Miss Wescott walked towards his parents. "I just think...she is so unlike you or he. She is so unpleasant and unsatisfied with everything except that which will indulge her wants and secure her ambitions...does he not see there are other women in Southamptons; in England? Surely there is one better suited to him!?"

Miss Dunsworth watched her a moment, then grinned, entwining her fingers with her friend's. "If I could choose for him, you know I would choose you. In my heart, you are my sister already." Isabel's heart soared.

~~~

The trees bloomed puce and gold and an All Hallow's Eve masquerade was held at Blackstone, with candles dimmed and sheer fabrics draped on posts and bannisters. Miss Dunsworth wore a deep purple satin overlaid in black and commissioned a mask and wings of raven feathers, Isabel fluttered about the rooms in ivory-colored peacock plumes, and Dunsworth embodied a ghostly spirit – dashing in white.

To Isabel Riley's great joy, Dunsworth asked her to join him nearly every other dance, and she did not trod on his boots even once. As she sat one dance out to catch her breath, a woman who's face she recognized faintly – but couldn't place – approached her and began speaking to her animatedly,
~~~

as though she knew her well. Through the course of the, mainly one-sided, conversation, it became clear that the woman had mistaken Miss Isabel Riley for Miss Miranda Riley, and was straightway put right.

"I confess am glad of the mix-up. I was at a wonder when you asked who I was, sweet as a lamb as you were, and quite took offense. How silly I feel now; although I can hardly be blamed as you are the mirror image of your sister. What a coincidence it is, to have your sister in our terrace in London some weeks ago, then come here and find you!"

"Yes, what a coincidence." Isabel smiled politely.

"My dear Victoria was very good friends with your sister. But you would know her too would you not? She was a guest at Tenby Hall this spring; with Mr Bradshaw and I, you most likely recall."

"Miss Victoria? Yes, I do know her a little. She is not here?"

"She is currently in Highcastle with a cousin of Mr Bradshaw's." This was said rather stiffly, as if Mrs Bradshaw was not happy about the circumstances of her daughter being there.

"Then you must give her my greetings when you see her next; and how long are you away from home?"

"Three weeks more.."

"A dance Miss Riley." Mr Dunsworth cut in with extended hand.

"Thank you, yes." She accepted happily. "So nice to meet you again Mrs Bradshaw, I hope you enjoy the rest of your stay in Southamptons."

Chapter 23

Behind Blackstone Abbey Isabel and Sicily ran laughing in fields of gangly trees, rained on by twirling, crunchy leaves as Eugene Dunsworth chased them, grinning, and demanding they return to him his hat.

"What is it the gentleman demands, Izzy! Do you see the gentleman's hat??" Sicily twirled and settled said hat on her friend's hair.

"I do hope he does not mean my hat!" Replied she, cocking it coyly atop her head, then dodging out of Dunsworth's way as he grasped for it half-heartedly.

He stopped, ruffling his hair and kicking the grass as he contemplated how to out-wit them – as if he could not catch them if he tried. He stepped towards Isabel, only for her to send the hat spinning towards Sicily, who caught it and placed it over her bonnet before dancing a little jig. Her jig was cut short with a squeal of glee as Dunsworth snagged his sister in his arms and attempted to force the hat from her hands; it was thrown over his shoulder and held aloft triumphantly by Isabel. His shoulders sagged with a sigh, though his lips still held laughter and his eyes still sparkled.

Dunsworth leaned against a tree, resolute. "I am bested." Relented he, gazing at Isabel from under cow lashes as he straightened his coat. She ambled over and held out his hat to him, but he saw the glint in her eye that told him her concession of his accessory was a trick. She did not retreat fast enough, and found herself pinned between he and the tree.

"Oh fie!" gasped she through joyful exertion. He plucked the hat from her fingers and tipped it onto his head where it belonged.

"I should have counted my blessings when I had only Sicily to bother me." Dunsworth declared with a pleased expression, utterly unbothered. He stepped back that Isabel might go free. "Now I've two wild things to live with and I am dreaming of the days I just had one."

"Pish Tosh! You love us! What fun would you have without us!" Sicily contradicted with a grin. "And don't say such things or Miss Riley with think herself a nuisance!"

"I hope Miss Riley knows never think of herself as a nuisance..."

"I shall try." Isabel obliged happily.

Mrs Dunsworths voice carried through the woods, "I am told you three are adults but am hard pressed to believe it! Come inside and get yourselves presentable or we will be late for dinner! Lady Fields will not be happy to be kept waiting!" They were not late, Lady Fields was happy, dinner was quiet except for murmured conversations and the occasional glance of silver against china; and the mewlings of Lady Fields' many cats. The Wescott's were there, naturally, as well as a visitor. Lady Fields' nephew, six-and-thirty years old, recently come home from the Americas, rugged and tan and very wealthy (Isabel was informed in hushed tones by Mrs Wescott that he had nearly seven thousand pounds a year). Isabel Riley ate her soup in inconspicuous silence and eavesdropped on the conversation between Miss Wescott and the man across from her.

"Are you happy to be back on English soil, Mr Fields?"

"Happy enough, but it's not near as exciting as the wild country."

"Oh La, I can imagine." her round eyes widened. "It must take a special caliber of man to brave such a place."

"You're right, there, Miss Wescott." he smirked. "You can't afford to be soft or you'll end up scalped or worse."

"Ooohh." Miss Wescott produced a little gasp. "Have you ever fought a savage?"

Mr Fields merely smirked again.

"How terrifying, your wife must worry for you every day." she simpered coyly.

"I don't keep a wife Miss Wescott. Life in the West is too rough for a gentlewoman." He once again smirked; Isabel wondered if he was capable of any other expression. Isabel also wondered how full of swill one man could possibly be, as she knew there were plenty gentlewomen in the 'West' who got on just fine. Isabel pushed a rather determined gray tabby off her lap.

"Life in the West sounds quite lonely." Miss Wescott was responding.

"One of the reasons I'm happy to be back home, Miss. After months with no company but that of a horse and the call of vultures, one becomes sore desperate for the company of a beautiful woman."

"Well I hope I can provide you with such company." Miss Wescott murmured without hesitation.

Isabel could not stop her head from jerking up to look at the pair with undisguised disbelief. Never had she heard such nonsense; and

Miss Wescott, who claimed some level of care and affection for Eugene Dunsworth, was lapping up said nonsense almost eagerly; nay, encouraging it!

In the dining parlor after dinner, Isabel sat with Miss Dunsworth and their matronly host, watching Mr Fields and Miss Wescott maintain their attentions towards each other; until finally Miss Wescott – with a playful flutter of her fan – let rise her voice just enough for Isabel to hear "La, Sir, you go too far, I shan't bear it! I am forced to seek more decent company!" and flounced over to settle at Isabel's side.

"How coarse and uncivilized that man is, Miss Riley, you will never guess what he just told me." She giggled secretively in Isabel's ear.

"I'm sure I am happier not knowing."

"Come, Miss Riley, let us explore the room." She spoke, standing again and taking Isabel's hand.

"I am well able to observe the general splendor from here."

Miss Wescott persisted with a tug on Isabel's hand. "But the details of the paintings and décor are much better enjoyed up close."

Masking her irritation with a small smile, Isabel gave way, allowing the girl to link an arm with hers and lead her around the edges of the room. "What do you think of Mr Fields, Miss Riley."

"I have not known him long enough to form much of an opinion. He displays generous amounts of exaggeration and arrogance."

"Oh la yes, but what man doesn't!"

"Mr Dunsworth is not arrogant, nor is he inclined towards hyperbole."

"Do you think him handsome?" Miss Wescott's eyes flicked towards where Mr Fields had sauntered over to speak with his Aunt and Miss Dunsworth.

"Mr Eugene Dunsworth is quite the most handsome man of my acquaintance." said she pointedly.

Isabel's arm was tapped in exasperation and Miss Wescott's eyes still remained on the man speaking to Miss Dunsworth. "Yes, yes he is, but I'm talking about Mr Fields."

"He is not below average, I suppose. He is very browned."

"You'll never guess what he just told me!" the girl tittered.

"So you have said."

"He was telling me more about the savages and I asked if it were true the men oft wore naught but a loincloth...and he said...he said he has one and wouldn't I like to see!"

"Why the devil would he have one??" Isabel sneered in disgust.

"Blessed if I know! I must admit I am curious though." was the sniggered reply.

"Don't be vulgar."

Miss Wescott's mouth sulked.

"I don't fathom your fascination with Mr Fields, I was under the impression you're in courtship with Mr Dunsworth." Isabel side-stepped a magnificent speckled long-hair who chose to gracefully prostrate itself in her path with a loud purr.

"It's not at all uncommon for a woman to have more than one man courting her at one time." Miss Wescott stated proudly. "It is better that way;

then one has options and can choose the man better suited, instead of having to take what one can get."

"I suppose love and constancy has little to do with it..."

"Sometimes I am at a loss with you Miss Riley, you are as strange as our Miss Dunsworth." the girl sniffed haughtily. "Any man who is handsome and wealthy is a man easily loved. And in any case, Mr Dunsworth is merely courting me, we are not affianced, there is no need for you to lecture me on constancy."

Isabel Riley no doubt would have been more understanding and amiable had she cared for Eugene Dunsworth less. As it was, she grew more furious with every word that fell from Miss Wescott's pouty little mouth. Isabel jerked her arm from that of her unfortunate companion and sought distraction before she said or did something regrettable. "Oh look, a kitten." said she, snatching the poor creature from its place of rest and removing herself from the startled Miss Wescott's presence to coo over and stroke Mrs Fields' youngest pet.

"It is time we take our leave, I think.." Mr Wescott was saying as she returned to the group, and Mr Dunsworth Sr agreed that they should also take their leave – much to Isabel's relief – as it was nearly eleven. They rose and acquired coats and shawls in preparation to set off, and at the door Isabel felt a hand on her arm.

"I am sorry if I offended you, Miss Riley, though I know not what I might have said. It was not my intention; I would hate to lose your favor."

"Oh, you said nothing offensive to me Miss Wescott. And pray don't make yourself anxious over losing my favor, one cannot lose that which they never had." She smiled pleasantly.

Miss Wescott's forehead wrinkled in thought, then her lip trembled and she whirled around to stride off stiffly towards her family's carriage.

"I am surprised at you Isabel, that was quite malicious." Sicily commented with a sympathetic look towards Miss Wescott, before lighting into the phaeton.

Dunsworth said nothing, looking at his sister as he lent Isabel a hand up. Isabel Riley endured an awkward and silent, albeit short, phaeton ride back to Blackstone. Once their feet touched the stone of Blackstone's courtyard, Dunsworth begged a moment with Isabel alone.

"I am aware you dislike Miss Wescott, Miss Riley, possibly more so than my sister; but I find it incumbent on me to request you try and be more kind to her. She did not deserve your derision tonight; I think you would do well to apologize to her."

Isabel clutched her skirts in agitation, feeling guilty, but also justified in her actions. "For what? Being honest? And I am kind to her! She winjes and complains constantly, and she insults your sister and I for pitiful little things such as wearing last year's fashions or wading..!"

"You cannot dislike her merely because she is sensitive and has a deep sense of propriety."

"Seriously? Really, seriously? I cannot agree. Miss Wescott is petty and a snob and you know it. She flirted with Mr Fields all through dinner tonight! You cannot be so blind not to have seen it.." She saw in his eyes and in the twitch of his jaw that he had noticed. "I do not see what it is about her that is so attractive to you; besides, perhaps, her ability to flatter men, and her well displayed bosom."

"You are being vindictive and crass." said he factually.

"No, please, tell me what it is that is so attractive to you, I wish to know; then I will apologize..." she begged. He said nothing, expression remaining passive. "Eugene Dunsworth, she does not love you, can you not see it?"

"I see it."

"Then why do you still court her!"

"I do not see why it is your business, but if you must know." His unruffled facade began to ruffle, his response weak. "It is because she is my equal; and she is sweet enough, we may grow to love each other."

"What? What?! That is the stupidest thing I have ever heard! Firstly, I will ignore your deluded belief that she is 'sweet'. Secondly, she is most definitely not your equal, in fortune nor in mind! She has not a penny to her name.."

"Of course, her lack of fortune!.."

"No! It is not her lack of fortune, but her want of it that does not recommend her!"

"And she is to be condemned because she does not wish to be poor and desolate in life!?"

"No! Please, refrain from willfully misunderstanding me! She does not suit you! You will not grow to love each other. She will use you, and you will grow to resent her!"

"None of this is of any consequence as we are not yet even engaged! Why do you take such an interest in my personal matters, how does it affect you who I do or do not marry!" Dunsworth snapped in frustration.

"Because I want you to be happy! To have Miss Wescott tell me she wishes to be courted by Mr Fields - among other things I shan't, for decency's sake, divulge - when you show her such loyal care and attention...it angers me to no end!"

Eugene Dunsworth considered this a moment, defeat and exhaustion settling on his features. "It should anger me. But it does not." He brushed a hand across his face. "It appears I do not care." They stood together quietly – and a little awkwardly – for some time. "Her interest in me is clearly not significant enough to commit her. This courtship was always destined to fail it appears."

"I am sorry."

He waved off her sentiment. "My heart is not injured. Only my pride. I thank you though, Miss Riley, I am flattered you care enough for me to be angered for my sake, I do not deserve it."

"You do. You are a good man and deserve to be loved for more than looks or money." assured she with utmost sincerity.

"You outdo yourself Miss Riley," he smiled wryly, and jokingly added "I will begin to believe you wish me to court you."

Isabel froze with her heart on her sleeve and she was not quick enough to hide it.

Eugene Dunsworth stared at her unmoving, smile fading and a look she could not discern entering his eyes. "Come, Miss Riley," offered he after a minute, thankfully breaking the strained silence, "it is cold outside, let me take you into the house where it is warm."

She moved ahead that he might follow her and not see her flush and flustered expression.

"Please be so good as to inform mother and father I will be out with my horses for an hour." Left he at the door. She nodded and hurried in as fast as she was properly able.

Chapter 24

Miranda Riley was consumed with boredom and melancholy.

Lord Riley seeing this, and understanding his company alone was not sufficient to cheer her spirits in the absence of her twin sister even with the added company of Matthew Westbrook, sent an invitation to his sister, niece, and nephew, and to Mr and Mrs Cotton requesting their presence at Tenby hall for a fortnight. After hearing his daughter mention offhand that a Mr Mastin had expressed a wish to court her with favorable results, Lord Riley thought it an appropriate thing to extend an invitation to this young man as well, with the intention of taking a measure of his worthiness. Thinking rightly that it would be a fine thing to surprise her, Lord Riley begged they keep it a secret from Miranda.

The day all were to arrive, Matthew took Miranda for a day of charity work, bringing baskets of goods to the poor. "I do love these days; and the weather is not unreasonably cold today either, splendid planning on your part Matthew!" Miranda chattered cheerfully as she tied up her bonnet and helped Matthew and the staff load baskets into the carriage. "It does one good to help others, nothing quite matches the feeling. It will be lovely going without Izzy for once, though I miss her terribly; she always carries on horridly about the poor souls' maladies and afflictions and makes the whole ordeal ever so depressing. Not that my heart doesn't go out for them, but there is no need to dwell on all we cannot do, when we are doing all we can. Oh! This trunk can be roped atop the carriage Mr Martin, it is just old clothing. Do you think it inappropriate of me to give away my old gowns and dresses, Matthew? They won't take offence to cast-offs, will they?"

"I'm sure the ladies will be thrilled with the opportunity to acquire quality attire at no cost, they will not think you pretentious because you do not give pretentiously."

"Very well, I trust your wise judgment. I do try not to be a snob you know, despite what Izzy thinks of me." She entered the carriage, holding a basket on her lap. Matthew followed, sitting across from her.

"I very much doubt Izzy thinks you a snob, Em. She just doesn't wish you to come across as one."

"She very much does think me a snob! You know she fancies the Dunsworth boy? I told her once or twice she could do better for herself, I could tell she was very upset with me and I'm certain that has solidified her opinion of me."

"I'd have to agree with her in that she would be hard-pressed to do better than he. Dunsworth is a decent fellow, and not destitute by any means."

"I have nothing against him. I just don't want Izzy to have any regrets in life; there is much she would have to sacrifice marrying someone with only two-thousand a year."

"He is worth over three- thousand in actual fact, much nearer four, not that that is of any consequence. It is admirable of you to care so for your sister's happiness, but consider this: if she really loves Dunsworth and does not marry him (given the opportunity) with respect to your advice, not only will she live with the greatest of regrets but she may grow to despise you because of it."

"...I had not thought of that."

Minutes passed; until Westbrook broke the silence. "What happened between you and that Mr Kirkley?"

"What??" Miranda startled, looking up to see he would not meet her eye. "Nothing, why?"

"No particular reason. I saw you and he were still quite close in London, I thought you might have come to an understanding."

"No! No, I don't think he is the type to attach himself to any one woman. Are you well? You look a little pale today."

"I am well. I am sorry, for your sake."

"Don't be. I was stupid. You know how silly I am about romance, and he played the part of a prince expertly. You did well to warn me away from him, Matthew, I wish I had been more receptive; it would have saved me an abundance of wasted time." She noted he looked as though he was struggling not to speak. "You have always spoken your mind with me; if you stop now, I will think we are no longer friends and will blame myself mercilessly."

He breathed a strange laugh, then inquired a little uncomfortably "It may not be my place, but, he never did anything...touched you.."

"Mercy, no! Thank heavens. He said a number of naughty things that I..I am ashamed..I did not discourage. I thought at one point during a crush at the Bradshaw's terrace that I...that I...uuh.." Miranda, obviously, had just been about to divulge that she had thought she had kissed Mr Kirkley, and that luckily it had not been him but a Mr Mastin...but then she realized that was really no better and, frankly, Matthew Westbrook was the last person she wanted privy to that information. "well nothing." she ended weakly. "Mr Kirkley did not touch me." Matthew looked as though he were in an immeasurable amount of pain and still could not look at her.

"Matthew are you really well?!" Begged she in alarm, forgetting the awkwardness of the conversation in her concern. "You do not look well in the least, we should return home that you may rest!" she raised her fist behind her to knock on the box and tell the driver to turn about, but was halted by Westbrook's assurance that he was indeed well enough to carry on. Once they were out and about, delivering goods and packages, their moods cheered.

Matthew watched Lady Miranda Riley chatter and laugh with the men and women they visited, or share a jovial look with him when particularly distrustful and bitter folks snatched the baskets' contents with barely a 'many thanks' or 'by your leave'. He smiled as Miranda cooed over the infant newly born to the village's young local beggar woman; and after they had moved on Miranda shared her decision to try and acquire a living for the poor girl, asking if he thought the beggar woman would appreciate the gesture or consider it presumptuous. He replied that regardless of what the young mother thought of the gesture, it was commendable of Miranda to take it upon herself to help them, and that with a child to think of the girl could hardly turn her nose up at the opportunity to earn a living should it present itself. Miranda was satisfied.

Their last stop was the orphanage, where the trunk of luxurious cast-offs was brought out and a beaming Miranda sat surrounded by twelve gleeful, laughing girls who gasped at and fondled the clothing, prancing and dancing about with gowns held against their thin bodies.

"I do love these days!" sighed she happily as they trundled home with empty baskets stacked around them.

"So I've heard." Westbrook replied with a crook to his lips.

"I don't think it could possibly get better than this except Izzy were back home."

"Would the arrival of friends suffice for now, in place of Izzy?"

She stared at him, searching his meaning. "You are filling her place well enough, but I always welcome more friends."

They carriage halted then, and Miranda looked out to exclaim "Why, we are at Thornhill! Do Papa and I have an engagement at yours which I have forgotten entirely?"

"Perhaps." drolled he vaguely, helping her out of the carriage and leading her in. The noise of chatter extended itself from a nearby grand parlor room and that is where they headed, Miranda looking now and then at Westbrook expectantly, with wonder and curious anticipation glowing in her features.

She gave a little cry of joy at entering, causing smiles and laughter to rise from the ten guests within. Miranda first greeted her Papa and Aunt and Uncle, before moving to embrace Miss Cotton and Cousin Charity, and welcome the others, including Mr Mastin; whom she did not expect - and secretly considered that when meeting a man one was in courtship with, one would expected one's heart to react with more than casual indifference. She tried not to think of the London kiss.

~~~

It was a lovely, increasingly cold, two weeks. Nothing of great interest occurred. There were pleasant walks during which one could see one's breath. There were cozy afternoons of cards and reading and piano-playing with vocal accompaniment. There were lively evenings of dancing and games.
~~~

Two things became abundantly clear to Miranda: She did not have any romantic feelings for Mr Mastin in the least; and, Mrs Cotton desperately wished to have her daughter set up with Matthew Westbrook.

The first was rather awkward as Mr Mastin still seemed interested in her, and though she did not wish to encourage him, she did not wish to seem cold either.

The second irritated her; irritation becoming a sort of panic or fear as she continued to try and ignore the emotion that had lingered within her surrounding Matthew, insisting it was love.

These two observations dampened her enjoyment and caused her so much unease that deep in her heart she resented Mr Mastin and Mrs Cotton and wished Papa had never invited any guests to stay.

The last night before the group departed from Tenby a suggestion was made. "Let us take one more walk together; I should like to explore Tenby one last time before we must go tomorrow!" Cousin Charity begged.

"It looks quite windy and gray.." Miss Cotton observed.

"But no so bad we cannot walk." Miranda countered, thinking some fresh air and time out of the constrains of the house might be good for her mood.

The others reluctantly agreed, voicing hopes it would not hail or storm. Miranda flew to acquire her warm outerwear and a bonnet, the others moving at a much more leisurely pace for their things. She stood eagerly by the door, tying her bonnet strings tight under her chin. "Oh no, but look!" Cried she as the butler swung open the door, letting in a violent gust of snow-laden wind that instantly coated the foyer with puddles and slush. The door was hastily shut.

"Look how the weather has turned, and only in the little time it took to acquire our coats! What terrible luck, we cannot venture into that!"

"I certainly hope it lets up before too long, else we may have to beg an extension of your hospitality." Mr Cotton commented worriedly.

"Oh, yes. We certainly can't travel in such weather." Mrs Cotton declared. "And the roads will not be safe enough to travel even after the storm passes, if it lasts much longer; so wet and muddy, the carriage will surely be stuck; and if it freezes! Heavens no, we shall have to remain for a few more days until the weather betters!" She finished, then added with a practiced smile, "If it would not be a burden on our gracious hosts, of course."

"No burden, I assure you, madam; we are well able to accommodate you all until it is once again safe to travel." Lord Riley obliged, removing his coat.

"Certainly." Miranda reiterated pleasantly, despite growing angst towards Mrs Cotton and her too-cheerful mood – it had not escaped her that the woman's gaze had remained on Mr Westbrook as she had been speaking of the state of the roads, clutching her daughter's arm. She laughed to hide her thoughts. "I, for one," bespoke she, undoing the bonnet ribbons she had just tied. "am not sorry to have my friends forced to stay. I am happy you are prisoners here for I was not looking forward to having you leave me tomorrow!" This was, of course, mostly untrue, but was said for the sake of keeping face and avoiding offence.

"We are hardly forced, Miss Riley." Mr Mastin grinned. "I dare say we would be well sorry to bid Tenby Hall goodbye tomorrow, more so than you would be to see us go!" The others were adamant in their agreement and Miranda schooled her face not to show her thoughts.

Said thoughts were interrupted by Edwin Lawrence. "I say – as our outing has been detained most rudely by this temperamental weather – that we retire to a sitting room for a game of cards!"

"Capital!" Mr Lawrence Sr clapped his son's back. Mr Lawrence and his son led the way with Lord Riley, Miranda took Grace Cotton's hand to walk together a little way behind.

"Truly I am glad of the weather if it keeps you here longer, Grace; it is so lonely here without Izzy and I am loath to part with you."

"As am I!" Miss Cotton smiled sincerely, giving her friend's hand a squeeze. "Though Mama is no doubt more exultant about the weather than I." she muttered more quietly.

After a moment's consideration Miranda determined it acceptable to pry, and did so in hushed tones. "If I may; are my observations from the past week correct, or is your mother not attempting to attach you to our Mr Westbrook?"

Miss Cotton flushed. "I'm ashamed she lacked the subtlety to hide it. I have been clinging to the hope it was obvious only to me."

"She would not be a mother if she did not try. He is quite possibly the most eligible bachelor within a hundred miles. Disgustingly wealthy, a reputable gentleman, quite handsome – an uncommon thing for a man to be all three."

"An uncommon thing for a man to be two of those together, far less three."

"Yes, he would be a fine catch."

"I'm sure he would," Miss Cotton sighed. "but he has no interest in me.."

Miranda's heart dropped. Had she been incorrect in thinking Miss Cotton preferred Edwin? Did she, in fact, care for Matthew?

"and I confess," the girl continued, looking away shyly, "my own interests lay elsewhere."

Miranda expelled her held breath, a hand on her heart with a small prayer of relief. "Your hopes are for my cousin then?" She begged.

"I dearly hope you are merely too perceptive," Miss Cotton's flush deepened, her hands rising to cool her cheeks. "or I will have been throwing myself at him!"

"I am merely perceptive. Fear not. I am glad, for now he will not be disappointed."

A startled expression shifted to one of hopeful cheer on Miss Cotton's face, but the question on her lips was hindered as Mrs Cotton's voice broke through their conversation. "Will you girls remain whispering in the hall or will you come in and share with the rest of us??"

"It is nothing interesting!" Miranda spoke quickly. "I just suggested to Grace that we play a duet, but we cannot decide on a song."

"Oh how lovely!" Mrs Lawrence smiled. "We are to be entertained!"

The girls sat at the pianoforte, picking a random duet. Grace Cotton whispered a secret thanks to Miranda as they picked out the first notes and began.

"Mr Westbrook, the ladies will need someone to turn the sheets for them." Miss Cotton tactfully suggested; but Miranda cut in before Matthew could rise.

"Nay, Mr Westbrook," began she, with a grin "we know you would rather remain in the company of men your own age, my cousin can assist us!"

"You'd best not be offended by that, Westbrook!" Lord Riley grinned as the other men chuckled heartily and Westbrook flustered. "I rather enjoy being likened to a man in his youth!"

Edwin Lawrence was already at Miss Cotton's side, and Miranda was grinning from the subtle and playful glare Miss Cotton directed towards her.

Chapter 25

As the evening progressed, Aunt Lawrence evidently grew tired of cards and songs and organized for an impromptu poetry reading in which everyone was to either write their own little piece to share, or recite a great piece universally known. Miranda, being well practiced in writing poems and ballads, thoroughly enjoyed the allotted quarter-hour of furiously pouring forth her thoughts in eccentric and passionate verbiage.

Aunt called time and they all settled near the hearth to read, or recite.Miss Cotton and Mrs Charity Bertram collaborated in a poetic debate – Miss Cotton praising serene winter, and Cousin Charity advocating for lively spring.Aunt Lawrence then read her pretty piece that flattered flowers in bloom.Mrs Cotton's little composition was a quite magical telling of a pianist bewitching her audience with soulful grace, claiming it was dedicated to her daughter. Miss Cotton thanked her mother shyly as the others commented on how lovely Mrs Cotton wrote. Miranda then took her turn, reading:

How despicable a thing is lingering youth; Though endearing and tolerable in it's rightful age, in truth, Naivete exposes inexperienced minds, and ignorance, that justifiable sin, Bares childish sentiment; And these, conspiring with stubborn denial, Build fear upon regret. Take care, for ravenous wolves with honeyed voices tempt. Beware thine own reluctance to give in to wisdom and sense.

She received a complimentary applause, much to the satisfaction of her ego. Matthew Westbrook's gaze lingered on her with indiscernible emotion; and, as her eyes met his, he gave her a small, brief smile before looking away. Miranda noticed then that he held a small paper in his hand and deduced that he would not, to her amazement, be reciting some well-known verse, but reading a composition of his own! That Matthew Westbrook might be the type to write poetry was something she had never considered; in fact, poetry was a pastime she would never have expected him to ever entertain, even if she had considered it! She was astounded, so overwhelmed with curiosity that she was hardly able to focus on anyone else until her anticipation was contented.

Her poem was followed by a recitation of William Woodsworth's Perfect Woman by Mr Mastin; he smiled subtly at her as the others commended him on his execution and memory; she tried to return his smile sincerely, knowing he meant the piece for her, but it had never been one of her favorites – too little character in Woodsworth's idea of a perfect woman, too easily applied to any. Her father recited a piece about daughters and she, as she was seated next him, leaned in to place a kiss on his cheek - he chuckled, well-pleased, and announced it was Westbrook's turn. Matthew Westbrook obliged with an operose clearing of the throat..

Oh sun; Ah no, Oh storm, For in clear skies does no such passion dwell. Oh wind, Oh waves, How fierce your tempest swells I fought the winds, oh foolish man, to capture or to tame, Ah mem'ry, Oh fleeting joy; She rent my heart and tore my very soul, what infant folly, to think sweet tempest be so readily gained.

Miranda stared, her rapture and wonder increasing with every line, watching his lips move as he read and every word causing her heart to swell until, the verse then over, it ached. The ladies gushed and men ribbed good-naturedly, while Miranda could only stare.She had judged him insensitive, unromantic; now behold how very wrong and how very insensitive she herself had been!Following Matthew's reading, Miranda could not force herself to listen with enough attention to even recall a word of those her Uncle and cousin Edwin recited.

Once the reading was over, and the general conversation following such an activity was spent, she took herself to the great library to find a novel that would suffice in distracting her from her mind's machinations. This was the library closest to the parlor the others occupied and she could hear their faint conversation as she ascended the iron spiral staircase up to the second tier of bookshelves. She was scanning through the third volume in her search for satisfactory reading material, when steps were heard on the iron stairs she had just taken.

Miranda did not feel unsafe seeing Mr Mastin approach, offering her a friendly smile, but her heart thumped uncomfortably and mind pricked with unease nonetheless. "Have you found something to your liking?" asked he, innocent of her discomfort.

Miranda comforted herself that Mr Mastin was no Mr Miles and she need not be afraid. Her unease fading, she returned his smile with her own genuine one. "I have, sir, I have decided on Shakespeare's Midsummer Night's Dream." She held it out for his observation.

"I have had occasion to read it. It is good fun that one."

"I have also read it before, but I should like to read it again. It manages to be both playful and solemn, both passionate and humorous; a difficult thing to achieve."

"No doubt." He drew nearer, leaning his head next to hers as he flipped it open to read "So we grew together, like to a double cherry, seeming parted, but yet an union in partition, two lovely berries molded on one stem."

She glanced up at him with a polite smile; a smile that faltered a little at seeing his eyes so near her own. He was very close. "It.." she swallowed. "It is a lovely passage..."

His eyes flicked to her mouth and she was reminded of the kiss in the garden. Her breath caught uncomfortably; was it about to happen again?? "May I kiss you Miss Riley." He asked softly.

Miranda wondered why she felt the urge to run. She had kissed him before and very much enjoyed it. She tried to muster up the same feelings now as she'd felt then; the ease and cozy comfort she had felt in his arms, the joy and contentment that had bubbled and shivered up within her, even his intoxicating, yet happily familiar, scent. But no, to her dismay, it was Matthew Westbrook's face that shimmered in her subconscious at the memory. Alas, Matthew would never love her more than a sister, she need set her sights on a more realistic goal. Mr Mastin deserved more of a chance than she'd given him these past two weeks, and she had kissed him already after-all, regardless of whether she still felt the same now as she did then.

She opened her mouth to give her consent but it would not come. The silence stretched on. He straightened a little. "I am sorry, Miss Riley, it was too forward of me."

"No I..I am sorry. I must be confusing you exceedingly after...after having allowed it in London."

His brows scrunched together. "Allowed what in London."

"Why.." Now Miranda's brows scrunched together. "Why in the hedge maze, when you came after me and you..and we.."

He was shaking his head a little, an expression of pure mystification on his face. "I do not follow. I never found you; I saw you leave, but I never saw you in the hedge maze, I returned to the terrace."

Miranda Riley's complexion faded to a ghostly pallor. "You did not kiss me that night...?"

He straightened fully, understanding in his eyes. "You mean to say, you kissed someone in the hedge maze in London and know not who it was?"

Miranda felt ill, faint. If it wasn't Mr Mastin, then who had she bloody well kissed!? Some arbitrary john off the street?! Her first kiss stolen by goodness knows who and she alone was to blame! How could she have been so foolish as to allow it, to put herself in the position for such a thing to happen! If anyone were to know she would be branded as licentious, a tenacious flirt, and oh how the hungry gossips would feast!

"I shan't tell anyone Miss Riley, but I think it would be best if we rejoined the others downstairs."

"Yes." She agreed shakily, thankfully. She knew by a glance that Mr Mastin thought less of her now, he would let the courtship die.

She did not feel a loss.

Chapter 26

They barely stepped into the parlor before Lord Riley called with a casual smile and gleam in his eye "Mr Mastin, there you are, I was about to invite Mr Cotton and my brother-in-law to go shooting tomorrow, would you like to come?" He gestured for the young man to join them in conversation. "My hounds are long due for a hunt!" Mr Mastin obliged.

Miranda saw Miss Cotton was occupied by a game of cards with her mother, Edwin Lawrence, and Aunt Lawrence, so she settled her focus on Matthew Westbrook who read a little way from the rest.

"Have you found tonight's novel?" Matthew looked up from his own, glancing between Isabel and Mastin's retreating back.

She walked to him and displayed the cover for his study, then sat in the chaise across from him and opened the first pages to read.

He watched her. "'O, when she is angry, she is keen and shrewd. She was a vixen when she went to school; and though she be but little, she is fierce.' That is a worthy choice, it suits you well."

Her eyes snapped up to his, her first instinct to take offense and retalia
te...but she was in a humbled mood this night, still feeling ill and trying
not to let the trembling in her fingers show, so he received naught but a
wry chuckle for his halfhearted tease before she returned to Oberon and
Titania in Athens.

Matthew knew her well enough to know her mind was uneasy; he tried
to cover his concern with playful jest, "Now, Em, what has you so pensive
tonight?" but was wildly unsuccessful.

"I am not pensive; I am myself, same as ever, unchanged." She laughed
lightly as she lied.

"I do not believe it."

"And I would like to read my book without distraction." smiled she, attention remaining fixedly on said book.

She felt his eyes continue to observe her, until finally with a sigh she once
again met them with her own. Where is the glimmer I am accustomed to?
thought she then I have not seen it in his eye a long while. Neither of them,
it appeared, were in the mood for cheerful banter these recent days. "And
what of you, Matthew, what of your pensive mood? I haven't been scolded
or made fun of in so long I shall begin to miss it." this was said genuinely,
not to be laughed at.

"I think I know you well enough to declare that false. You shan't miss it in
the least." He focused on the book which he held in his lap, remaining too
long on one page to convince any one he was reading it.

"And I declare you know me little if that is your understanding." She
huffed, a little irritated. "I put on a great act, but in my heart, you should
know, I quite enjoy it..the teasing I mean. The scolding I don't enjoy, but I
am not too self-righteous to admit the task needs must be done regardless
of how unpleasant it may be for me, especially with Izzy now away."

"I will quit Thornhill soon, you will have to depend on Lord Riley to scold you."

Her book closed firmly and she demanded his meaning.

"You know I have acquired and renovated a townhouse in London, I thought it might be a natural thing to assume I may make it my permanent residence. I mean to take permanent residence there in two weeks' time."

"So soon?? Why have you waited until now to tell me?!" at his annoyed gesture towards the others she recalled they were not alone in the room and lowered her voice. "You cannot leave on such short notice! You should not leave at all; you belong at Thornhill!"

He attempted to comfort and explain. "I'm not about to give up Thornhill, I shall return often; but I must move on with my life at some point."

"Move on with your life?! You are not content with us?? Are we not enough for you??" Her words came out as a hiss in her attempt to remain quiet, she did not wish to share the argument with the small party on the other side of the room.

"What in blazes are you on about! You know I love you girls and your father like family, but I cannot remain a lonely bachelor at Thornhill forever! I am nearly thirty-one, Em, I must..I cannot.." He trailed off, unsure of how to speak his thoughts, unsure if he even should.

He means to seek a wife! Miranda was attacked by a vicious wave of panic, her breath becoming shallow and quick. She could not allow it to happen! She would not entertain the thought of him charming and wooing the simpering ladies and debutantes of London! He was too rich and would be surrounded by conniving money-chasers and light-skirts who would not even try to love him for more than his money! This was all her fault, if only she'd allowed herself to love him sooner. If only she had not been so stupid and flirtatious and deceived herself! She began to see spots and tears pricked her eyes.

"Miranda!" Her father's voice cut through her conscious, voice sharp with concern. She responded weakly. Her father seemed to hear her. "What happened Matthew! Did you say something? Did she express any concern of illness??"

Matthew Westbrook had acquired a ghostly pallor. "I..I do not know..she just went blank.."

"Take her too her room, my sister will come with you to help get her settled into bed. I'm going to speak with the cook, or perhaps it is too hot in this room."

Miranda forced herself to come to her senses. "I am very well Papa, you are right, it was too hot in this room that is all, and my corset..I have been feeling ill all day." lied she.

Her Aunt followed her to her room, watched over her as her abigails relieved her of her crushing corset, dressed her in her nightgown, and tucked her into bed. "Aunt.." Miranda called as Mrs Lawrence was about to leave her to rest. "I was speaking to Matthew about an urgent matter, if you would be so kind as to send him up.."

Mrs Lawrence's brows crashed together. "He didn't distress you did he? Was he the cause of this.."

"No, Aunt, he did nothing, but I would feel better if I could speak with him." Her Aunt was unconvinced but obliged her niece's request. Matthew tentatively entered and set himself on a nearby armchair.

"Em, are you really ill or did I.."

"I am not ill.."

"Then I beg you, tell me what it was I said to elicit such a response that I may apologize and remedy my error!"

"Gracious how dramatic you must think I am! I just..I really do not wish you to leave." one tear escaped her eye as she expelled a short laugh at herself. He gazed at her in amazement with something akin to pain in his eyes. "Why do you stare at me so." laughed she again, warily.

"You shake me, to my very core, I know not what to think." uttered he.

Her expression fell and froze, her brain sputtered.

"What is it?" He rose and stepped toward her. "do you feel faint agai.."

"No! No, I am fine I just..I need to think." She thought hard about the day of the Bradshaw crush. That day she had seen Matthew leave the dress shop. The old shopkeeper there had said – in regards to the fine suit of gothic visage with the embroidered velvet waistcoat – that the gentleman had ordered it for a crush that was held that evening. She knew that gentleman was Matthew, she also knew she had seen Matthew briefly at the crush that night, leaving early. He, then, had been there and had been in a velvet waistcoat; he was a good head taller than her and styled his hair long enough to run one's fingers through... "Matthew," began she, tentatively, "I saw you briefly at the Bradshaw crush in London, as you were leaving; did you happen to see me at any point that night?"

Neither of them spoke, Matthew Westbrook began to look positively ill.

"You didn't happen to be in the hedge maze at all did you?"

He did not deny it, looking more ill.

"Did you..was it you who.."

"Stop." he choked.

"I do not want for any more miscommunication! I must know!"

"Merciful Lord." He sank back into the chair, digging his hands into his hair.

"Please Matthew; did you kiss me?!"

He made a sound like a wounded man. "Yes."

"Oh. Oh Matthew I am so relieved; but why?" Begged she hopefully.

"Why?? What manner of man you must think am! I would not touch a woman I did not love with all my heart!"

"Then...you love me, as a woman, not a sister." she breathed; her own heart full to bursting.

"I have for some time, and now you see why I must remove myself from Thornhill."

Her heart cracked. "What?? That is the greatest reason not to go!"

"You wish me to remain here, in agony, watching you flirt with, and be courted by, other men?! Have I so grossly underestimated your selfish vanities?!"

Heavy tears rolled from her eyes. "And have I so grossly underestimated your capacity for sense?! Why is it, do you think, that I am so distressed at the thought of you abandoning me to find yourself a London wife! Has it not yet occurred to you that I love you?"

"I cannot be satisfied with that, I will always crave more from you than brotherly love. You cannot fathom how difficult these past months have been; my guilt, anger, even physical pain - I cannot endure it, I am sorry, Miranda!"

Miranda Riley recalled, at that moment, the words that had caused him to flee the garden after their kiss, and shame and horror covered her face. Matthew had loved her then; she could imagine the overwhelming joy he must have felt at her encouragement and reciprocation – and then, oh wicked woman, she had called him Kirkley – spoke of ravishing - she now understood the true meaning in the poem he had read earlier this evening; for truly, she had rent his heart and torn his soul that night, with quick and merciless efficiency! If she had been in his position in that moment..she could not fathom. Miranda crawled atop the covers to kneel before him on the edge of her bed, crying bitterly into her palms with profuse apologies as she begged his forgiveness.

Not being made of stone, and still being in fervent love with her, Matthew approached to wrap her tightly in his arms and assure that he had never felt wronged and so there was no need for forgiveness. To this she replied (becoming calmer in his embrace and breathing in an intoxicatingly familar scent she could now identify as Matthew's) that she had, in fact, wronged him abhorrently; and that she did not deserve his care and empathy in this matter, that she deserved a scolding. He enlightened her to the knowledge that he need not scold her this time as she was doing the job well enough herself.

After a moment, once her sniffles had subsided and eyes mostly dried, he all but pushed himself away from her (much to Miranda's despondency) and ran his fingers through his hair (for the twentieth time that hour) with a ragged sigh.

"I wish you would have held me a little longer." lamented she.

"Miranda.." he breathed a forced, agitated laugh, "I have expressed what my feelings are towards you, you have been witness to - nay a victim of – those feelings unchecked. Why do you insist on testing me? Do you think me made of marble?? Do you enjoy watching me tortured??"

"Evidently I have not been clear enough as to where my own romantic affections lay.."

"I know where they lay, I implore you not to tell me I cannot bear to hear it." He begged angrily.

"Honestly Matthew, you are as bull-headed as they come. If you are thinking of Mr Mastin allow me to correct you for he is not the one."

Matthew dropped himself into a chair and rested his head on his knuckles, his features pale with exhaustion.

"This is not the way." Miranda muttered to herself, rubbing her aching temples. "We are both too weary and overwrought to make or understand any sense. Let us rest tonight, gather our thoughts, and resolve this tomorrow morning. Will you walk with me to the duck pond, at eleven o'clock?"

Despite a subtle wish to decline, the answer was "Very well. Goodnight then, Em." and he left the room.

Miranda Riley tucked herself under the blankets, tossed, turned, and barely slept.

~~~

There were blue skies the next morning when she woke at half-past ten; she dressed quickly in a warm baby-blue muslin and acquired a thick cape - it was chilly despite being sunny. She wandered in the direction of the duck pond - now devoid of ducks - and soon caught sight of her Mr Westbrook striding towards her. She offered him a little smile once he joined her, they walked in silence. The pond was blanketed in a thin film of ice, smooth, transparent surface marred by delicate frost. Miranda sat on the stone bench and patted the space next to her, Matthew Westbrook obliged.
~~~

Nerves caused her to hug herself tighter as she mustered the courage to say what she had come here with the intention of saying. I should have just said it last night, it would have been easier in the moment thought she apprehensively. She began. "When do you think it was that you first began loving me, as more than a sister or friend?"

He gave in after a moment's hesitation, not meeting her eye.. "...I think...in the spring during you and Izzy's presentation ball," he clenched his jaw, then his hands. "when I first saw you in the white gown."

She dropped her gaze to her own fidgeting hands. "That same week, while we sat in the early morning and watched the ducks, do you recall?" he inclined his head in the affirmative. "It was then that I discovered I cared for you more, so much more, than as a dear family friend; it was then I realized I loved you, as you now profess to love me. I only wish I hadn't ignored it; I wish" she swallowed, "I wish I had not been so caught up in the fantasy of romance that I nearly ruined myself; and much worse, I caused you unnecessary pain, caused you to lose hope - and for that I shall never forgive myself. I only cling to the hope that I have not injured you so deeply that I cannot convince you to remain with me...or at the very least, allow me to follow you, wherever you choose to go the remainder of your life. Even if it means leaving Tenby." Her speech ended, she sat in silence, terrified of his response.

Miranda felt his fingers intertwine with hers, she held her breath.

"You've stolen my proposal, love."

She rose her eyes to his, the expression in his causing rapturous tears to spring up in her own. "I suppose it follows you ought to give me an answer." She beamed, her vision watery.

"I require no convincing, I will remain at Thornhill if you vow to remain there with me, as Mrs Westbrook."

"Oh mercy! How odd that sounds - Mrs Westbrook." laughed she.

"Lady Miranda Westbrook." tested he with an incandescent smile. "I rather like it."

Squeezing his hand happily she requested "You must call me that as often as you are able so I may get used to it." They were grinning at each other, her gaze lowered under her lashes humble and shy. "Matthew, dearest; as excessively delicious as our first kiss was, the circumstances were neither ideal nor proper. Would you mind, terribly, kissing me again now I know it's you?"

"Would I mind??" smirked he, cupping her face and leaning his forehead against hers to speak softly, "Why, Mrs Westbrook, it would be my greatest pleasure." before complying to her request.

Chapter 27

Had Izzy been home at Tenby the two girls would be excitedly planning for the younger twin's matrimonial festivities.

Alas, Izzy was not home, therefor Matthew and Miranda were forced to postpone their impending nuptials until her safe return.

Snow drifted down upon Southamptons, blanketing the sleepy flora and fauna in a delicate blanket of flurry. Isabel Riley and the Dunsworth siblings were visiting a public park; enjoying the general glittering splendor of the outdoors, breathing in the icy air and laying tracks in the newly fallen snow. As they walked, they were hailed by someone behind them; they turned to find Miss Wescott leaving the company of her parents to catch up to their little party. The three walkers plastered on smiles as they waited for the girl to join them.

Isabel, who had been trying these past weeks to mend Miss Wescott's injured feelings, welcomed her kindly and complimented her hooded cloak, expounding that she would have her seamstress create one just like it for herself. This pleased Miss Wescott, she believing herself quite the setter of trends. They conversed about the weather, the joys of winter, and which seasons were their favorite and why.

Sicily Dunsworth, thoroughly bored of the polite, societal conversation, rolled a crunchy ball of snow and sailed it towards her brother's back, garnering a very satisfactory response – an exclamation of surprise and displeasure as he hurriedly brushed the dripping ice from under his collar. He had whipped one back towards her before any of the three of them had a chance to react. Sicily ate the snow from her stinging cheek with a glint in her eye towards Izzy. Izzy discerned the meaning of this glint and exacted revenge on behalf of Sicily. A war ensued.

"Stop! Oh do please stop!" wailed Miss Wescott. "I hate snow-fights!"

"Come now Miss Wescott," Dunsworth turned on her. "Are you so averse to a little fun?" Sicily and Isabel stared at each other with raised brows.

The lady pouted. "It is so wet, and cold. I will be made wet and aggrieved."

"Your cloak is heavy, and protects you well; we will go easy on you I swear it." He grinned at her, tossing a ball of snow in his hand lightly.

"I shan't join you, I don't think it any fun at all. I shall sit on this bench if you would be so kind as to brush it off for me, and shall watch from there."

"Very well." agreed he with a smile. He strode to the bench Miss Wescott had pointed out, gave it one mighty, unceremonious swipe with an arm, then jogged back to his sister and Isabel – who stood and observed him with keen interest. Miss Wescott gaped, offended by his slight, and slumped onto the cold, wooden seat with barely concealed displeasure.

"I give to the count of sixty for you two to fill your stores with artillery, then we shall have a proper battle." declared he with a confidant smirk, already gathering balls of packed snow a few yards from them.

With a cry, Sicily and Isabel began forming their own spheres and piling them behind a tree trunk. Dunsworth called time. The battle broke out and the players entirely forgot about poor Miss Wescott sitting forlornly nearby until, eventually, a wayward missile streaked through the air toward her and landed quite smartly on her collarbone. She jumped up and squealed in such distress the other three thought she might have lost an eye!

"It has only hit her chest." Dunsworth said in relief once he and the other girls had inspected the damage. "We are terribly sorry Miss Wescott, I suppose we let our game run a little out of hand. I hope you will forgive us?"

"Has only hit my chest??" bewailed the damsel. "How insensitive Mr Dunsworth, Sir! It stings and is dripping freezing ice down my décolletage! Why must you oblige them their silly games instead of sitting with me?"

"I quite enjoyed our silly games, I was under no obligation."

"Well I am fed up with them, I am going to find Mama and Papa!" threatened she.

"I hope they have not gone far." replied he sincerely. "I will walk with you. I won't be long Sicily, Miss Riley, wait for me." He offered Miss Wescott his arm and started off.

Sicily clutched Isabel's hand once the two were far out of hearing distance. "He is telling her their courtship has come to an end, I am certain of it! Did you see how he neglected her? He acted almost himself – playing snow games with us in the stead of sitting stiffly with her.." she joggled Isabel's hand a little, enthusiastic. "Do you not think?"

"I think...I cannot say, but I feel you are right. I am sorry for Miss Wescott, if he is ending it."

"You are not." Sicily stated matter-of-factly.

Isabel laughed a small sheepish laugh. "I am not so lacking in compassion that I cannot be a very little sorry for her."

"That is fair. I believe you have played a pivotal role in his change of heart, Izzy."

"Hardly. It would be more accurate to credit Lady Fields' nephew for that; in any case, we both know his heart had little to do with it, it was more of a change of mind."

"True on both accounts, you are you are quite wise for so young a person Miss Riley."

"You are aging yourself with that comment." Isabel was playfully smacked. "But in seriousness, nearly-nineteen is not so young; and I am far from wise but I thank you for I know it was a sincere complement."

"What is taking my brother so long."

"It has barely been three minutes, you are shockingly impatient. They do not know where Mr and Mrs Wescott are."

"Let us go to that pretty bridge yonder and see if the river is frozen over."

"Likely it is. It is not so much a river as a rather ambitious creek."

"If you are still here at Christmas-time, I wonder if it would be plausible to have your family come to Blackstone for the holidays."

Well used to Miss Dunsworth's conversation jumping about from topic to topic in quick succession, Isabel took it in stride. "I don't see the harm in it. I would love to show them Blackstone, and I believe the danger of another Frightening Encounter rather unlikely after so much time has passed. Likely the-man-we-shan't-name has fled the country."

"Likely." agreed Miss Dunsworth. She brushed the snow off the wooden railing and they peered over at the running water below. It was indeed covered by a thin layer of clear ice. "Pretty." She commented. Isabel nodded with a smile. Sicily then pulled herself up onto the thick rail and began to walk it, arms out for balance.

"Sicily! Oh please do be careful!" Izzy cried, readying herself to catch her friend lest she fall.

"I am perfectly safe, see?" Sicily chortled and terrified Isabel by turning quickly on the rail and running along it on her toes. She hopped off. "I have had lots of practice, Eugene and I do this often. You try."

"Are you not afraid??"

"I used to be a little, but no longer. I will help you!"

Isabel gingerly lifted herself to kneel on the rail, clinging to Miss Dunsworth's hand tightly. She stood and took a wavering step; then another steadier one. Isabel walked from one end to the other, thrice, both girls giggling and hooting every time she made it across.

"I should like to try without the help of your hand...but stay very near me!" Isabel declared bravely, smiling wide. One foot ahead of the other she made her way along. She neared the middle.

"Ah look, Eugene is finally returning."

Isabel halted a moment to glance up and see Dunsworth some way down the path jogging towards them, calling loudly. "Miss Riley, you are endangering yourself! Sicily what have you encouraged! Have her down from there!"

Isabel began to join Sicily in protest and continue walking, when a distant figure in black at the edge of her vision pulled her attention; the figure stood motionless, watching. Fear gripped Isabel Riley in its claws, her step faltered and she tipped. "Isabel!!" Mr Dunsworth yelled, bolting into a hard run! Ice shattered. Freezing water enveloped her, blurring her vision, filling her throat. She struggled to stand in the waist-deep water but her limbs failed her.

Then, she was ripped from the water into warm arms and carried to the bank. A fleeting sardonic thought at least I am awake this time was overwhelmed as cold numbed her brain. She blinked up at Mr Dunsworth, trying to speak through useless lips. "I t-t-thought, I t-though I s-s-s-saw.."

"Sicily my cloak." Interrupted he, biting out the words against the chill as he relieved Isabel of her sodden one. "Blast this cold."

Sicily handed him the cloak he'd thrown at her as he flew over the railing. He draped it over Isabel's trembling shoulders and fastened it tight around her. "Run and tell the carriage to be made ready with haste."

Sicily obeyed. Dunsworth began to lead Isabel in the same direction but, when it was proved she had no command of her feet, soon swept her up once again and hasted towards where they had left the family carriage. He shook her, "Come now, don't fall asleep on me. Look there, our chariot, we will be in the warmth of Blackstone Abbey soon."

"Y-you are wet t-too." she commented, concern in her sleepy features.

"Only up to my hips, no need for concern on my part." Her eyelids drooped, opened as she was sat in the carriage and it lurched forward, then drooped once more. "Sicily she is falling asleep!"

Miss Dunsworth clutched her friends arm and gave a gentle shake. "Stay chipper a little longer dearest, we will soon have you in a hot bath with steaming tea and a warm fire.." Isabel smiled, her tense shivering beginning to wane, eyes drooping further.

"That was little help, you've gone and relaxed her further."

"What else am I to do!" his sister snapped.

"Isabel, what was it you were trying to tell me? You said...you thought you saw something?"

Isabel's eyes snapped open. "Yes! I saw a f-figure watching us. It terrif-fied me, it is what m-made me s-s-slip. I was af-fraid it was Lord M-Miles."

There was a shocked silence. Though the threat of Lord Miles finding Izzy had always been in the back of their minds, time had diminished it significantly. The threat was now, once again, made very real.

"Are you confident it was he.." Sicily begged.

"I cannot be c-certain, he st-tood too far away t-to make out his face; but I fe-feel..I have the feeling.."

"I am inclined to trust your intuition." Dunsworth decided. "I will tell father and mother, we will have to be more cautious."

They arrived home. Isabel Riley was whisked into a hot bath in front of a fire and a cup of tea thrust into her hands by Miss Dunsworth.

For three days Isabel lay confined in bed very ill; and was diligently attended to by every member of the Dunsworth family. The fourth day she became delirious. Their Doctor suggested they summon Miss Riley's immediate family with the expectation Miss Riley may not last the week. The Residents of Blackstone Abbey were desolate. Sicily Dunsworth sat by Isabel Riley's bed, stroking her hair and applying cool cloths. Sicily's father entered, coaxing her gently to retire as it was very late. She assured him she would soon. Some time later her brother entered and placed a hand on her shoulder. Sicily broke into ragged sobs.

"It is my fault Eugene. I wasn't watching her, I wasn't holding her. I should not have led her into such a precarious situation in the first place!" Eugene wrapped his sister in his arms.

"You cannot blame yourself for such a thing. Isabel is capable of making choices for herself, you did not force her up there; and hear, she said it was the mysterious figure that caused her distraction, all would have been well if it were not for that."

"You are kind to me brother. I cannot be so kind to myself."

"Hush, I will watch her for a time. Go rest, cease your regrets and have hope, our prayers may be all that can save her now." Miss Dunsworth let out a small wail of anguish from behind the kerchief pressed to her face. She fled to her room.

Dunsworth stood alone in the dark room, lit only by the light from the hall. He took the seat his sister had left vacant and leaned in to watch the young woman swaddled in blankets before him. A sheen of perspiration decorated Isabel's forehead and cheeks, her breath rattled and she fussed in her sleep – muttering for Papa and Em. She pulled one arm out and pushed at the blankets as though she wanted them gone, so he reached to turn them down and offer her some relief. Her eyes drifted open, her hand touched his face, lips muttered his name. Eugene froze; then her lids closed and hand dropped.

Eugene Dunsworth's heart broke. He knelt to lift her hand with both of his, to entwine her hot, mucid fingers with his own, and spoke in quiet desperation. "Do not leave us Miss Riley, I beg you; your sister and your father are on their way, stay strong, for them; you will see them again!"

He held their clutched hands to his brow for a long while. "I would give all my strength, my life-breath, to have you well again."

A raven flew past the window and dove into the trees, startling a silent walker in the woods.

Chapter 28

The following afternoon welcomed Lord Riley, the younger Miss Riley, and her espoused to Blackstone with grey skies and solemnity. Miranda Riley and Sicily Dunsworth, though they knew each other little, fell on each other and shed bitter tears before rushing upstairs with Lord Riley to be with their beloved ailing Izzy.

Miranda and their father spent most of the next day and a half with one on either side of Izzy's bed, holding her hands tightly in their own. Hope grew as over the course of this day and a half Isabel's breath grew clearer and cheeks increased in their color; until finally, her fever broke, eyes opened, and she spoke - a little weak and raspy but spoke nonetheless.

"Em, you are here."

"Yes!" Em cried tears of joy, kissing her sister's face. "And Papa, and Matthew!"

Tears also flowed from Lord Riley's eyes as he kissed his daughter's hands and cheeks. "Praise the Lord, my Izzy, we thought we might lose you!"

"Oh." Sighed Izzy, with a weary smile. "I am so glad you are here."

They spoke quietly together for some time, updating Isabel on the general goings-on at Tenby and coaxing tidbits of conversation from her; until she finally asked. "Where is Matthew?"

Matthew was immediately called, and Miranda asked her father if she and Matthew could speak to Isabel in private for a brief moment. He obliged.

"Izzy, this may not be the best time...but I know you would be angry at me for holding off on you.." Miranda began, taking Matthew Westbrooke's arm and pulling him close.

"Please be about to tell me you two are engaged..." her twin murmured with a smile.

Matthew laughed outright. Miranda flushed. "Yes..we are. We have been for some time now but had no way of telling you.."

"Oh I am glad." Izzy closed her eyes with a sigh. "Where are Eugene and Sicily?"

"That was a highly anticlimactic and disappointing reaction." Matthew smirked.

"Shush, Matthew," Miranda patted his chest, grinning. "She has not been awake a full hour yet and is exhausted. They are just outside the door, Izzy, dearest, and quite eager to see you. I shall call them in for you."

"I am so glad you've come; you two, and Papa. I've missed you all terribly."

"And we you, Love. Now, we will let you alone with your friends, but only for a moment - that's all I can bear. Come Matthew." Miranda ushered him out and spoke to someone quietly at the doorjamb. Eugene Dunsworth peeked around the door; seeing her roused and colored and gazing at him, he entered.

"How do you feel? Can I have anything fetched for you?"

"I ache all over and find myself awfully thirsty. But I feel much more myself; thank you."

Dunsworth had already gestured for a maid to acquire water for her. "You will do well to get some proper rest."

"I feel as though a good stretch would do me better."

"No doubt, but there will be none of that for a day or two yet."

"I shall take that as a challenge I hope you know."

Dunsworth grinned down at his hands. "I should have known better."

"Izzy! Oh you are awake finally! Oh we have been fair distraught with worry!!" Sicily burst in, brandishing something before her. "Behold, honeyed crumpets! We have barely got anything into you this past week, I implore you, eat!" The siblings helped Isabel sit up and laid the plate before her. She obediently picked up one of the glazed delicacies and nibbled off a bite.

"Ah, wonderful, she is eating, splendid!" Miranda clapped, re-entering with their father (who came bearing a pitcher and glass of water) and sitting on the bed next to her sister. "Eat up, eat up, Izzy, we shall have you out and about in no time!"

~~~

They did not allow her to rush her recovery, but despite their best efforts Isabel was still striding around the house and laughing over games with her friends and family before a full week had passed; not quite so cheerful and lively as her usual self, and her appetite had shrunk; but nevertheless, the doctor was impressed with the rapidity of her improvement.

On a particularly sun-shiny winter's afternoon-nearly-evening, nine days after her she had woken from her fever, she donned her cloak and bonnet
~~~

with the intention of walking Blackstone's trails and watching the sun sink over the pond.

"Where do you think you go this eve young lady?" Mrs Dunsworth halted her. "You'd best secure some company if you are venturing outdoors, we do not wish you snatched off our very land."

With a chagrined blush Isabel twisted her fingers. "That is quite improbable I'm sure, but" she conceded, "I suppose you are right to be careful. I shall call Papa."

Papa acquired, she hurried outdoors; but was veered away from the path that led to the pond. "I think it is best we stay near the house; we will circle the courtyard."

"Nay! Must we Papa?! The pond will be so prettily iced over, I wish to see it!"

"It is still too far for you yet, you would tire, and I would prefer you walk the trail with a group earlier in the day for the sun is now drooping in the sky as though it wishes to set. Mrs Dunsworth is good to caution you, this Lord Miles may be patient and calculating."

"I would much rather think him stupid for my own peace of mind."

"Let us speak of pleasanter subjects. The Dunsworth's are a fine family, they have treated you well?"

"Very well." She smiled brightly. "Mr and Mrs Dunsworth are so jolly and kind and accommodating. Sicily is wonderful, every bit a sister to me; she has made it a little easier on me to be parted from Em these past months. Mr Eugene Dunsworth is.." Isabel found she had no words, suddenly bashful beside her father.

"You have cared for that boy for some time." her father smiled a little, then he laughed at the look on her face. "My daughters' fancies are something I tend to keep a close eye on."

"He is not a boy. He is very much a man." muttered she, growing red.

His laugh faded to a grin. "You need not fear I disapprove of him. I might have had some scruples in years past but I gladly put them aside once he was compared to your sister's choices.."

"Ah yes, I had heard a little of her behavior; and she divulged every detail of her season to me during the few days I was confined to my bed. I am glad she had the sense to love Matthew for there is no one better suited for her. She needs guidance, and a great house to manage and fill her time with. She will love being the mistress of Thornhill."

"Yes, there is no union that would have pleased me better." Lord Riley chuckled. "I declare you could really do no better for yourself than Eugene Dunsworth, Izzy; the only potential mark against him would be if he is unwilling to take the woman without the forty-thousand pounds."

"I beg you do not test him, Papa, I know what you are thinking! Don't you dare pretend to take my dowry from me, how cruel you are!" Isabel laughed with her father, then, continuing more seriously, "No, he is too honorable for that. It is more likely, I think, that he will never ask for my hand due to the belief that he would be unable to make me happy."

"Do you think him able to make you happy?"

"The man himself, yes, absolutely." She flushed hard. "Monetarily - I believe so, I am determined not to be so superficial as to let it dissuade me. His family makes four-thousand a year?"

"Approximately; three-thousand-five-hundred or more.."

"That is by no means poor."

"I agree."

"And with the added monetary advantage I would bring to the marriage I would not have to give up luxury...which is something that, if I had to, I would not be averse to giving up."

"And you know I will always be able to provide you with help if help is needed."

She pulled her father in to kiss him on the cheek. "I doubt that will ever be necessary, Papa; but yes, I know you will."

"Right then, I am now set to the task of making friends with this lad."

"Oh dear, I hope you do not frighten him."

"Heavens no, I will be pre-emptively welcoming him into the family."

"Ah! Papa! But that will frighten him, certainly!"

"Have no fear, I will merely be very civil and approachable, with the intention of allowing him a little more ease at the thought of asking me for your hand."

Isabel sighed. "This is all weighing on the assumption that he wishes to offer for me."

"If he hasn't fallen in love with you in all the time you've been here at Blackstone, then I question his sense and you're better off without him."

Isabel's lips twitched into a smile. "Spoken like a truly loving and loyal father. Em and I are lucky to have you." They walked for a short time in affable silence. "I grow chilly, you were wise to keep our walk short, I am glad we are nearly back at the house."

Lord Riley conceded it was wise of him indeed, as snow had begun to drift softly to the ground; and once they found themselves in the soothing heat of the indoors, they then found themselves some tea and pastries.

Chapter 29

Miranda had brought two of her lady's maids with her and lent one of the girls to Isabel for the duration of her stay. The young girl helped Isabel Riley undress, laid out her clothing for the next day, and waited for Isabel to enter the bed that she might blow out the candles. "I will blow them out myself, Ruth, I wish to watch the snow fall before I go to sleep." Ruth nodded and left, shutting the door behind her with a faint click.

Isabel blew out the flickering candles to let the silvery-blue moonlight wash through the room. She watched scattered bits of fluffy white float gently past her window, until after a few minutes it stopped snowing altogether and the air glistened. To her delight she could just barely see the pond from her third-floor bedroom, and it mirrored the moon splendidly, a sheen of ice, like crystal, coating it's surface. She sighed in happy satisfaction.

Something at the bottom of her vision caused her to move her gaze to the small garden clearing at the back of the house. A figure in black, stark against the white snow, stood staring up at her window. Isabel remained frozen in fear, her vision tunneled in on this dark, unmoving visitant!

Stars blinked in and out of her line of sight and she realized she had ceased breathing! Taking two great, shaky breaths, her brain awakened and she fled the room!

"Goodness heavens you gave me a fright!" Miranda whispered laughingly as Isabel dove beneath her twin's blankets.

"Miranda, I am absolutely certain I just saw Lord Miles out behind the house, in the gardens."

"Dear Lord and Savior! I pray you are mistaken! What on earth was he doing??"

"Nothing. Just standing there still as death, fixed on my window!"

The girls clutched each other in terror. "We must tell Papa and Matthew, and Mr Dunsworth, and perhaps Mr Eugene Dusworth. If he is there now then they may be able to catch him."

"Oh no, Oh must we?? Never-mind that is a silly question I know we must." They quickly rose, donned thin house-coats, and rushed to their Father's room. After a quick account of what Isabel witnessed, Lord Riley rushed to rouse the other men. There was a rapid and silent scurry for pants and coats and horses they the four men shot off to the back of Blackstone to chase down the skulking stranger.

The four women huddled tightly together by the front parlor fire, waiting for their return. Ten minutes passed.

A noise at the front door caused their hearts to race, it was creaking open slowly. Four pairs of eyes widened and breaths stilled.

"Hullo! Back already?" Mrs Dunsworth called loudly, not letting her nerves weaken her voice.

"That certainly didn't take you long!" Miss Dunsworth added, putting a finger to her lips lest the twins endeavor to speak and potentially encourage the trespasser by hearing Miss Riley's voice.

The door creaked closed and faint footsteps jogged down the front steps. The ladies rushed to the large bay window to peak through the curtains, a lone figure of a man, hair pulled back in a thick stallion tail, was racing across the courtyard towards the woods. Mrs Dunsworth expelled an unladylike word and ran to the back of the house to yell for the men. The other three let loose their held breaths and began expressing desperate wishes that the four who had journeyed out to catch the unwanted visitor would turn about and chase him down; but alas, they remained on the opposite side of the house, out of sight and, apparently, out of hearing!

It was an hour and a half before they returned, saying they had tracked fresh prints through the back woods on a wide and meandering path to the front where they had found horse prints, and then the trail was lost. At hearing Lord Miles (whom they assumed the stranger to be) had nearly entered the house, Lord Riley, especially, was fraught with anxiety and frustration.

"We must always have one of us in the house at all times!" Lord Riley declared vehemently, and cursed, "He was in the house, the audacity of the man, the boldness! If we had only returned sooner! If only we had not gone first to the back of the house, we could have had the bastard! I'm sorry.." he turned to the ladies, feeling guilty for his language. Miranda and Isabel wrapped their father in their embrace, comforting him, and themselves.

Mr Dunsworth Sr hugged his wife and daughter briefly in turn, expressing he was glad they had the sense to speak up and scare him off, and more so he was glad they were safe. Mr Eugene Dunsworth sat by the fire looking sick and gazing often at Isabel with worry in his eyes. He spoke up. "I concur we must always have My father, or Lord Riley, or myself at home. This was too close a call, we have not been considering the risk of Lord Miles seriously enough. There must be some way to trick him, to bait and trap him."

"We have no proof it was Lord Miles, none of us saw his face."

"We saw his hair was long and tied back, in the fashion Lord Miles wears."

"That is something, but we need mo-"

A loud clearing of the throat and tentative "Do 'Scuse me, Miss Riley..er m..Miss Isabel, ma'am." The maid shut her mouth warily as all eyes rested on her.

"Yes, what is it Hilly?" Mrs Dunsworth beckoned.

"A letter, fer Miss Isabel." the girl stepped tentatively into the room, presenting the letter for their inspection.

Isabel rose and took the letter, "No sender." then settled back into the armchair with her sister to read. She managed the first two lines before snapping her head up and demanding. "Where did you get this??"

"Ther by the door Miss. On the letter table."

"It is still damp, and I need only read the first two lines to know who it is from." All eyes were now on her. "I do not wish to read this, Sicily, can you read it for me?"

Sicily acquired the letter and looked as though she were about to read out loud, but "Oh, but this is lunatic!" she sped through the remainder of the letter. "It is signed. Your Beloved, Bartholomew Alexander Busic Miles...He sincerely believes you are in love with him! What nonsense! Some of this is quite inappropriate!"

"Well then, there is our proof." Eugene gestured with a wide sweep of his arm.

"We most definitely need to contrive some sort of plan to capture him, he is guileful."

"The plan of action I can see as most likely to be successful is to bait him, and we know who would be the most tempting bait." Matthew looked to Isabel for confirmation.

"Absolutely not, we will not force Miss Riley into danger." Eugene snarled.

"Stand down Dunsworth." Matthew reasoned. "I was thinking she might send him a letter, I would never risk putting her in his presence."

"That is very good, how shall she contact him."

"In the letter he claims she should leave him notes in a box he has hidden in Windsdown park, by the bridge in which she fell.."

"Oh I knew I saw him there that day! I knew it was he, my instincts caused me to fear him immediately."

"Superlative instincts." Miranda muttered.

"Then we shall leave him a note." Eugene agreed.

"Saying..?" Mrs Dunsworth asked.

"Perhaps that Miss Riley wishes to meet him at an inn or park, then we can surround him." Mr Dunsworth Sr suggested.

"Better to send him into a carriage, then we can lock him in." Isabel countered.

"Capital." Eugene grinned, as Sicily added.

"Yes! and we can have a constable inside dressed in a lady's cloak and bonnet!"

"Rather unnecessary details those." Matthew raised a brow.

"Necessary, actually. Do you wish him to see a constable as he enters and jump back out prompt? Or see a lady at first glance and sit down before realizing his mistake?"

"Very fair point." Lord Riley agreed. Matthew added sardonically. "Unfortunate there aren't any lady constables to complete the illusion."

"Lady constable!" Mrs Dunsworth exclaimed jovially. "What a notion!"

"This seems to be our best, immediate, course of action." Mr Dunsworth Sr stated decidedly. "If Miss Riley would be able to finish a letter this night?" (Miss Riley nodded, she would) "We will take it to this hidden box or what-be-it on the morrow."

"It is morning." Sicily muttered as Lord Riley and Mr and Mrs Dunsworth retired. Isabel moved to the letter table and the others grouped around her.

Miranda was speaking, "You will have to write quite convincingly, Izzy, love."

"Convincingly? Can I not just write 'I have received your note, let's run away, I'm sending you a carriage at such-and-such place at such-and-such time' and be done with it?"

"Nay! Isabel, we can not afford to do thing's half-way. He must be sure you wish to run away with him, or he may be suspicious and not show up."

"Merciful Mary! Am I to conjure a pretty essay pretending to hold undying affections for the man? It is unthinkable, I am repulsed by the thought!"

"Not an essay, merely a paragraph." Miranda sighed, exasperated. "Just imagine you are sending a note to someone you do hold undying affections for!"

Isabel failed to keep her eyes from flicking toward Eugene, and was mortified when his crystal blues met her own. Idiot she scolded herself with a blush. "Could you not write it for me Em? You were always better at writing eloquently and prettily than I."

"Oh very well." her sister sighed. While Miranda wrote, the other four hovered over her, helping with the more specific details.

"Friday, four o'clock." Suggested Matthew. "It gives us time to prepare, yet is not so far away that he will grow restless and attempt to contact you again. And it will be darker in the evening, better to disguise the figure in the carriage and hide those surrounding it."

"Very good." Dunsworth agreed. "I just had the thought, is it likely our Lord Miles will be watching this hidden box?"

"Likely." Matthew concurred, raising a brow in question.

"Well if he sees one of us men dropping off the letter he is bound to suspect foul play against him."

Sicily agreed "Then we will require Izzy to place it there herself."

"Are you daft!?" Eugene responded angrily. "We cannot let her alone in his presence! She will be plucked away before our very eyes!"

"Unless you wish Lord Miles to flee, Mr Dunsworth, that may be our wisest course of action." Isabel contradicted gently. "Although I would not go alone as it would be inappropriate, you know this. I will just have to find some excuse for searching under the bridge, without him coming to the realization that my company is aware of this box."

"This is becoming over-complicated." Miranda sighed, finishing up the note.

"Yes; but we cannot take any chances, he must be caught." Isabel spoke with fearful desperation in her voice.

"Of course, Dearest!" Miranda cried, turning on her stool to wrap her arms tightly around her sister's waist. "Lay your fear to rest, we will catch Lord Miles and he will be locked away in an asylum for the rest of his days!"

"We will not allow a repeat of The Frightful Encounter, Miss Riley." Eugene assured. "Every measure will be taken to ensure your safety."

Isabel was surrounded by love, she felt the welcome relief that poured over her, spirits lifted and nauseating anxiety lessen; she was grateful for it, even if it was only a little relief, even if only for a moment.

She slept with her sister that night, tossing fitfully. She dreamt of hollow-eyed ravens swarming, dreamt of drowning and frigid waters blackening with their depth. Lord Miles, grinning lasciviously under a dead gaze, reaches for her. She cannot take his hand to save herself, she does not wish to; the panic of breathless lungs soothes and she dances in silence in the dark, Eugene Dunsworth warm in her arms. Her vision then blurs, jitters, Eugene's face contorts and she is in the arms of Lord Miles. His arms crush her that she cannot escape, cannot even scream. She opens her eyes to see the delicate fabric canopy over her lavish bed at Tenby. Isabel rises and glides to the window to peer out on the night scene below. A dark figure stands there watching. Like a phantom of death it flies at her; and she stands deaf and dumb, paralyzed in place as it engulfs her sight and stills her lungs. She stands at the window to peer down at the night scene below. A dark figure stands there watching. Silent and quick it flies at her; and she stands deaf and dumb, paralyzed in place as it engulfs her sight and stills her lungs. Again she stands in the window, and again a dark figure stands below her, watching. It flies at her over and over until finally she wakes, gasping and throwing off her sheets to cool her shivering limbs, coated in a sheen of sweat.

"Izzy!? Are you well?!"

"I am well, Em. I had a bit of a nightmare is all."

"A bit of a nightmare...Dearest, you're positively trembling.." Miranda slurs sleepily, then clutched her sister's hand and pressed an arm around her until they both returned to a heavy sleep.

Chapter 30

Walking tightly between Miranda and Matthew, Isabel Riley clutched a small purse to her chest, a small purse containing The Letter. As they neared the bridge in the centre of Windsdown park her eyes darted unceasingly to the shade laid by trees, and the paths winding through and around the park, searching for any figure that looked as though it may be watching with sinister intent. She took deep breaths to calm herself.

"What shall I do? How shall I hide it in a way that seems secret?"

"You could drop something and tell us to go ahead." Matthew helped.

"O-Ok, yes. That seems a sound plan." Isabel's eyes looked to her twin's in trepidation.

"We will remain on the bridge for you, we will not go ahead; we will not abandon you, Izzy."

Isabel nodded. They attempted to force a cheerful conversation, and, as their feet brought them onto the bridge Isabel stepped forward, laughing, and flung her arms wide (startling Em by nearly hitting her; she apologized with her eyes) letting her purse land below on the river's edge.

"Oh dear!" Cried she loudly, "You have caused me to lose my things in my exuberance."

"Dramatic but effective." Matthew muttered in surprise. Miranda was speaking over him. "Never mind, go back and retrieve what you have lost, we shall wait for you here!"

With the urgency to be done with the uncomfortable task, Isabel rushed back down the bridge and down the steep little embankment to the sliver of rocks that bordered the small river she had fallen into a few weeks before. She did not immediately see any sort of box.

Isabel turned to venture into the dim shadows under the bridge and found herself facing none other than Lord Miles himself! She stifled her scream.

He smiled lovingly, tenderly, reaching a finger to her lips and his other hand beckoned her to approach. Glancing up she could see the backs of Matthew and Miranda turned to her. Isabel had the immediate thought to call to them and have the man seized in that very moment but a gleam caught her eye. The man had equipped himself with a pistol!

A mere second passed in which Isabel's mind worked at a frenzied, adrenaline-induced speed. He would not try to abduct her here, in public, in the light of late morning; and if she called for help he may behave rashly and wound, nay kill, someone. Act! Coaxed she to her terror-stricken self. ACT! She forced a shaky smile and crouched to join him under the bridge; brushing her fingers to his but not having the stomach to actually take his hand.

"What are you doing here, you may be caught?" whispered she as quietly as possible, trying to hide the repulsion in her voice with a smile and hoping it was dim enough that he would not see the insincerity there. She added, "I thought there would be a box.."

"No box, I surprised you did I not?" returned he cheerfully, then, "My beloved Isabel, you need not fear for me." spreading a hand across her cheek with his words brushing her jaw. "I have remained undetected from these fools for an age. I thought I had lost you; but lo, I overheard Lady Bradshaw in London telling how she had come upon you here...Lovely Angel, it was as though you had sent her; you had begged for me and look, but our prayers have been answered and fate has aligned for us!" She attempted to remove his hand from her face but his fingers roped tightly around her wrists, stopping her. "I feel you tremble for me as I do for you my sweet pearl, do not contain it. Trust we shall be together soon, for all eternity."

She opened her mouth to speak, and there emerged naught but a strangled whimper. She tried again. "I-I must return to my sister...lest she discover us. H-here, I have written a letter; for you." She scrambled to procure it for him. Lord Miles moved with snake-like speed to kiss her lips; she moved with equal speed to dodge it. "Oh merciful Mary! I mean. My Lo-" she gulped. "My Love, I could not until our," she wheezed "wedding day."

His eyes widened, he grasped her hands and pulled her to his chest. "You are too pure. Yes, my Angel, my Life. Now go!" He snatched the letter. She fled.

Miranda and Matthew observed the expression on her face with bewilderment; her features contorted in fear and eyes shining with unshed stress-induced tears. She shook her head at them while attempting willfully to produce a steady, cheerful voice. "Let us finish our walk! Now then, Em, do continue telling me the stories from your London season!" and as they rushed away from the bridge at nearly a jog she begged in hushed tones "Go! Go! For heaven's sake, go!"

It was not until they were safely in the Blackstone carriage that Isabel divulged what had just transpired. And then back at Blackstone Abbey she was obliged to re-tell her story. The brazen-ness of the criminal, the shocking fact that he carried on his person a pistol! The threat of danger from Lord Miles was greater than they had predicted!

~~~

The house waited in heavy anticipation for Friday evening; then, when the time came, the five ladies waited with Mr Dunsworth Sr for the others to return with the news of Lord Miles's capture.

It was late into the night when Lord Riley returned with Matthew Westbrooke and Eugene Dunsworth; they appeared drawn and tired, evidently wishing to be seated comfortably before divulging any details. Eugene, immediately meeting Isabel's expectant eye upon emerging from the night into the entry hall, allowed them all relief by speaking softly, "it is done."

The details were divulged thus: They had stationed plain-clothed constables, and themselves, inconspicuously around the area. The carriage had arrived, an armed man within swathed in a cloak, no bonnet. Ten minutes in approximation had gone by when Lord Miles appeared, hailing from the opposite street, and approached the carriage hesitantly; then rushed it, all but diving within by all accounts. The carriage had been immediately surrounded and a wild clamor had erupted from inside. The door was opened, firearms drawn, when shots began to blast through the air, two in succession then one a few moments later. Lord Miles had shot the man in the carriage after a scuffle (the man was shot through the thigh Lord Riley assured, not a fatal wound, but another man was not so fortunate). Lord Miles briefly thereafter realized he was caught; he shot again, missing Matthew very closely and grazing his ribs (this information bringing forth a short cry from the twins more than the others, and Miranda rushed to inspect him), hitting the man behind him in the chest. That man did not survive. Once Lord Miles came to the realization that his beloved had betrayed him, and that he would undoubtedly be imprisoned and later
~~~

hanged for murder, he turned the gun on himself and pulled the trigger before he could be stopped.

A long silence hung in the room after this account was over.

"Well," Sicily broke it. "As morbid as this may be, I am glad of it. We are safe from him now."

"We are safe." Isabel repeated, staring into her steaming teacup.

"It is late. We all need our rest." Mr Dunsworth Sr flipped closed his pocket watch. The others agreed.

~~~

"It seems odd to just go to bed after a night such as tonight." Isabel confessed to Miranda under the blankets of her sister's bed.

"I dare say for those who were witness to the event, it is more so. How traumatic to see two men die so climatically in one evening, one after the other."

"Yes, I cannot imagine. Poor papa, poor Mr Dunsworth."

"Poor Matthew."

"You are safe now though Isabel."

"My mind is not convinced; it doesn't yet seem real; though I suppose no part of the events these many months has felt real."

"Believe it Izzy. There is most evidential proof for you to believe in, in any case. You trust Papa and Matthew..and Mr Dunsworth. Every time you look on one of them you will be able to think to yourself 'there, they ensured my safety, they saw with their very eyes the end of my cause for fear'."
~~~

"That is very macabre assurance."

"I know. I am sorry. It was badly said indeed."

"Not badly said; in all honesty you are correct. I know it will be a long while before I feel safe and secure in life without one of them nearby."

"You will be able to come home now."

"Beloved Tenby, how I've missed her. I cannot wait to see those marbled walls and painted ceilings once more!"

Chapter 31

One week found the Riley family back at Tenby Hall. The twins and Matthew Westbrooke began wedding planning immediately, the matter of the date being decided on first thing; conclusively: mid-July.

They spent one day meticulously inspecting a few nearby venues, returning home as the sun began to sink below the horizon. While Miranda, and Matthew heatedly discussed their options with Lord Riley and debated on where they would most wish to be married, Isabel wandered a few steps behind, her gaze settled on the great pillars that led up to the cathedral ceilings of Tenby's massive front hall; oblivious to the others entering one of Tenby's many sitting rooms, Isabel stood in the hall looking up at the clouds and cupids dancing above her, deep in thought.

What was the reason for having murals so high above that one cannot even make out what is painted there, besides naked body parts and the occasional ray of plaster sun? The empty echo of feet on marble as a maid hurried by caught her attention. Isabel didn't recognize her, the girl must be new, or service a part of the manor Isabel did not frequent. How large Tenby was, there was no doubt fifty rooms or more that she had not stepped foot in more than once in her whole life, if even that many – was it odd to be unfamiliar with much of one's home? It felt odd, all of a sudden.

She resumed removing her bonnet and wandered towards the parlor where the voices of her family emerged, a man standing by leaned forth with the express purpose of opening the door for her – she had never noticed him before – what a singular profession. A strange sadness filled her, a tedious loneliness that lingered even as she accompanied her twin on the setee and joined in on the conversation.

Isabel Riley soon came to the realization that Tenby Hall now felt less like home than Blackstone Abbey; and it was a realization that concerned, nearly frightened, her; for she could not go back again for quite some time without insulting her family and presumptuously inserting herself into the Dunsworths' lives.

She desperately missed the abbey, and more so Mr Eugene Dunsworth; it was likely that her love for the place largely derived from her love for the man. A thought in her mind overwhelmed all others and she pulled aside her father to ask him quietly.

"Papa, do you recall the conversation we had in the courtyard at Blackstone regarding Mr Dunsworth."

"Yes."

"Did...Did he ever speak to you?"

"He did not; not that circumstance ever promoted an opportunity."

"Yes. True." Isabel sighed. "...I am going to visit the gardens; I feel the need to take some air."

"Very well, shall I come with you?"

"My thoughts will be ample company, thank you Papa." She smiled. She trotted outdoors but did not make far before her sister linked arms with her.

"I will not allow you to brood alone. Come, tell me what is on your mind."

Isabel opened her mouth to answer.

"I'll wager you're pining for your Mr Dunsworth aren't you?"

Isabel shut her mouth.

"I must apologize, Izzy, I have always belittled the Dunsworths and discouraged you from forming any sort of permanent attachment to their family...but now we quite owe them, for preserving your life.. thrice over! They are a lovely family, and I underestimated their worth greatly, for they are very fashionable and I was not left wanting at any point during our stay at the Abbey. I give you leave to marry him and, in fact, I encourage the match!"

"Very well and good. All that is left – this is something I find myself repeating often of late – is for the man himself to wish to marry me – and evidence of that is not substantial."

"I am certain there is very substantial evidence. No doubt you are merely moping. Here, I have an idea that may cheer you, let us ask Papa to invite them to Tenby for Christmas, yes?"

"Absolutely not! You will do something embarrassing to thrust us together!"

"No! I am thinking it would be wonderful for us to have Sicily here for Christmas!" She looked sideways at her sister.

"I suppose so, we always have Aunt and Uncle Lawrence, and Cousin Edwin; but ever since Cousin Charity married, we have not had feminine company nearer our own age over the holidays. Yes, let's ask. Let us ask immediately so as to give them time to respond and prepare!"

~~~
~~~

Mr and Mrs Dunsworth responded very favorably. Their family was pleased to have received the invitation to stay for a week as special guests at Tenby, and were very willing to accept. Time moved too slowly for Isabel, who dearly anticipated the arrival of a certain young man over any one else.

On the set day of everyone's arrival, Aunt and Uncle Lawrence received a happy welcome from both twins at once, Cousin Edwin a slightly more polite welcome, and the Dunsworths an overwhelmingly joyous one.

After embracing Sicily and Mrs Dunsworth, Isabel discovered she was uncommonly shy with Eugene; unsure of whether to offer her hand, give him a small curtsy, or merely greet him. The first seemed to pretentious, the second very strange indeed, the third she decided on but ended up standing before him awkwardly and saying nothing.

He saved her by speaking first, much to her relief. "I did not think I would see you again so soon."

"And yet here you are. You could not bear to be parted from me." Joked she.

"Nor you from I, I hope." Smiled he, adjusting his hat by the rim, and turned to greet her father.

Isabel stood dazed a second or two while she processed his comment. Why realized she with rapidly lifting spirits that was quite flirtatious! Then she was swept into the cheerful company of Sicily and Miranda, and she forced herself to minimize the number of times she let her infatuated gaze wander in the direction of Eugene Dunsworth.

Like a twitterpated youth of fifteen years she swaddled herself in her bed covers every night that week and giddily wrote in a diary every encounter and conversation with him that caused her heart to hope.

December twenty-one. Everyone is now settled down for the night early. It has been a long day of travel for all those who had need to, luckily the weather was mostly fair, with only the slightest bluster. We had a pleasant enough dinner; I did not sit next to Eugene. Miranda and I made sport with Mr and Mrs Dunsworth for they cannot for the life of them tell us apart. Miranda answered to my name and I to hers and we had them so well fooled that even Sicily, Edwin, and Uncle began to mix us up. Matthew ruined the illusion for he was unwilling to play the part of my fiancée – I laugh now thinking of it. I appears Eugene has no difficulty telling us apart; I know this because during our charade I noticed he was often aiding us in our game in order to confuse his poor sister. I know he was not confused himself because whenever he would lie to Sicily 'No, that is Miranda, not Isabel' or tease her with 'One would think after so many months with her you would know her face' I recognized the glitter in his eye and the curl in the corner of his lip as he looked at me. I am so incomparably happy.

December twenty-two. Today we went riding. The sky was full blue, the sun blinding, the air so full of frost it froze our lungs; I loved every minute of it. I noticed he often moved his horse to remain near mine, but perhaps it was just his horse – for the horse we gave him is one of my favorites and may be used to receiving carrots from me. Miranda complained a little and Aunt turned back before too long with Mrs Dunsworth. Eugene commented many times how the young steed we lent him – my favorite, Odin – was an exceptionally handsome Friesian and very strong etc.. It is not fully broken in and he expressed that training horses is a hobby of his – which I know very well – and how he would love to work with 'fine stock such as this'. I have asked Papa secretly if I may gift him one of our Friesians – Odin in particular – this holiday and I have been given consent. I believe horses are a great investment; I don't believe Odin will be too inconvenient or thoughtless a gift; there is a large, well-fitted stable at Blackstone and I know Eugene has an exceptionally good understanding of horses. My nerves are showing. I digress.

December twenty-thee. Today was exceptionally busy, we went to town to do charity work. I formed a group with Sicily and Eugene (because Eugene requested I join them, I please myself with the theory that this is a sign of affection) and had a splendid time giving out baskets of baked goods, blankets, and other necessities. Sicily has a shamelessly charitable nature and as I watched her tuck in old Mrs Mills and feed her soup I felt humbled and ashamed that I had so much less care for the comfort of others than I thought. She has inspired me to do more than put baskets of food on the tables of the poor, I will endeavor to make their lives easier in other, more personal, ways. I expressed this to her on the ride home and she told me I must not belittle my own kind efforts, that I had done the most and she was merely trying to do her little part to contribute. If I knew her less I would be inclined to think of her as falsely modest and self-righteous – but I know her good heart well and I could only think those things of her out of spite for wishing I had an equal or better character. I also praised Eugene for his compassion and willing labor, for he showed a character similar to his sister's while we were at the Mills'. Mr Mills is far too old to be cutting wood and his struggle in this task was sadly evident upon our arrival at their small farm; Eugene, despite the cold, removed his overcoat and began splitting logs for the gentle Mr Mills while we were inside the small one-room farmhouse. Papa has commented on occasion that Mr Mills is too old to be laboring so, but even Papa has not deigned to pick up the ax. I do not know a better man than Eugene Dunsworth. Eugene was exhausted, the scent of outdoors and wood hung about him still once we returned home to Tenby and I quite liked it (no, I did not go about sniffing him). He retired early. Miranda told me, before leaving my room a half-hour ago, that Eugene should not have 'chopped wood' as it is unseemly for a gentleman to do such things. I told her Matthew would not consider himself above the task and she had nothing to say to that.

December twenty-four. Today was rather uneventful, we played a variety of card games and Eugene wished to be my partner any time a partner was required, claiming I was the cleverest lady in the room; he said it to tease his sister and mother but I took it as a compliment nevertheless and hid my pride and joy behind a laugh. I have not yet had the chance to gift him Odin. Cousin Edwin left for London quite unexpectedly this evening, I know not why, but Matthew seems to know and Eugene seems to have an idea, I am all curiosity.

Chapter 32

December twenty-five. Today we did feast. I tried to glean from Matthew the reason for Edwin's sudden departure but he was as giving as a stone wall. Lunch is over and, every last one of our party now bloated and languid from excessive gluttony, we have retired to a sitting parlor and croaked and sat about like frogs in a muddy hole. I sit as far from the heat of the fire as I can and write. No one wishes to speak more than a sentence or two, undoubtedly due to the discomfort of talking with stomachs taut.

"What is it you write so fervently?" Eugene Dunsworth's voice interrupted her flow of thought.

She snapped her journal shut and turned from the writing desk to face him. "Nothing of great interest, just an account of the day."

He placed a small chair quite near her and sat thereon. "Nothing of great interest is still something of little interest, and better than nothing at all - which is what I have been doing this past hour. Might I succeed in coaxing you to read it to me or shall I be scolded for prying?"

She quickly skimmed her eyes over her current passage and, determining it was safe to read aloud, she smiled, "Very well, for the sake of your sanity I shall indulge you." she read him the December twenty-fifth entry.

He chuckled. "I would not call that only a little interesting, I found it entertaining. Will you continue writing or will you indulge me further with your company?"

Isabel's smitten heart could have burst. She complied. He returned his chair back to it's set in the corner of the room and she joined him there.

"You wouldn't happen to know the reason for my cousin's sudden departure would you?" she tried her luck at prying information from him considering she had been unsuccessful with Matthew all day. Dunsworth claimed he did not know the full of it but gathered it had somewhat to do with pursuing a lady.

Isabel imagined her cousin had decided on a whim to see Miss Cotton, he had been displaying the marks of one with an attachment to the lady of late. She did not mention this to Eugene Dunsworth; instead she joked "My cousin has not been away from London a week! How desperate some young men are in their pursuits that five days is too long to be parted from their lady love."

"You claim you cannot relate?" jested he with a grin.

Isabel could, of course, relate to some extent; but what was she to say?! "Every woman has been crossed in love at least once, and it therefore follows I can."

Then he teased further saying "At least once? Is it to be assumed then that you have fancied more than one member of your opposing sex?"

To which she replied the negative "I am unfortunate in that I have only ever loved one." As the words left her mouth she feared she had become too brave; but something brightened in his eye causing her to begin to understand why Miranda loved to flirt – if that is what one would call the exhilarating sensation in one's chest that threatened to steal one's breath; though thought she I am only bold enough to do so with Eugene, I don't understand how Em mustered the audacity to flirt with so many strange men.

"Why is it unfortunate to have only loved one? That shows great loyalty and strength of character."

"I feel it shows more foolishness than any such things as you claim. I am infinitely more likely to end up with a broken heart than any number of ladies, such as Miss Wescott, or even my sister.."

"A broken heart is one thing I am sure you will never suffer Miss Riley, I do not think any man you desired could refuse you his heart."

She searched his face for anything that might suggest some hidden meaning or hope, but he wore a passive protective mask she could not see past. She had broken this mask before, she wished to do it now. "The man who holds my heart is proving to be one such man."

"Perhaps then he is not worthy to hold it."

"I find him worthy; my father considers him worthy; and if he has any strength of character then he too will see himself worthy."

Eugene Dunsworth looked momentarily lost for words. Then his polite mask returned as Lord Riley spoke next to Isabel, causing her to jump. "Dunsworth, what do you say to a hunt tomorrow morning early, before you and your family ride home?"

"I am certainly not oppose to it, Sir.."

"Capitol. And if you have no other plans this afternoon, would you be willing to tour our stables?"

Eugene Dunsworth was eager, nearly animated, in expressing his willingness. Lord Riley then lent a pointed look to his daughter. "You would join us, Izzy?"

"Yes, I would." spoke she happily, and more quietly in his ear as they exited the room, "Thank you, Papa." He replied with a wink.

~~~

Young Mr Dunsworth and Lord Riley conversed for quite some time over the animals and breeding and livery. Isabel cooed at the horses and whispered in their ears, stroking their forelocks and feeding them sweet dried corn in the palm of her hand. Her father caught her eye after quite some time, and inclined his head discreetly in a gesture for her to come closer. They were nearing Odin's stall and Dunsworth had recognized the fine beast. Nervously Isabel approached and spread her fingers into Odin's shining ebony mane.

"You have splendid taste Mr Dunsworth; Odin is my favorite here at Tenby, out of all this years' foals."

"Absolutely beautiful, no doubt; and a hearty spirit. He will be a strong and loyal steed to whoever ends up his master."

"You could be his master...if you wish."

Shocked, Dunsworth looked to Lord Riley, who nodded with a smile.

"I already asked Papa, I would love for you to take him, if..if you wish."

"He would fetch you a great price, I cannot just take him from you!" Dunsworth protested, but his eyes betrayed his excitement and want.
~~~

"You would not be taking him." Isabel grinned, knowing he could not resist. "We are giving him as a gift. Come now, you would not risk offending us with your refusal?"

He relented easily, with a wide smile – something rarely seen on his face. "I would not dare, Miss Riley, Lord Riley, I cannot express the measure of my gratitude. I shall gladly ride him back home tomorrow, Odin will be the pride of Blackstone."

"Why wait to ride him?" Isabel suggested.

"Yes! Let us mount and take him for a run, Dunsworth." Agreed her father.

Dunsworth visibly struggled to curb his enthusiasm. "Yes! Yes, why certainly. I'm sure they could use a stretch of their legs. The others won't miss us if we are not too long. Where is a hand?"

A stable hand was called over to prepare Odin and two other horses and they were soon cantering across white fields.

"Ah look, there we see Thornhill, Mr Westbrooks home." Isabel called, and pointed towards the towering manor as they peaked a shallow hill.

"Fantastic." Mr Dunsworth called back, sincerely impressed.

"Miranda will soon be Mrs Westbrook and will be mistress of it, well occupied in her time."

"No doubt. It will take quite the woman to manage a manor so large."

"Yes...quite the woman indeed. My sister will be well up to the task, I would not be able to say the same for myself.."

"I am certain you would pull through well enough." smiled he with a twinkle in his eye.

She smiled at him. "Perhaps; but I cannot say with certainty I would be happy to. I would have to spend far too much time indoors and that would drive my sanity from me. Even Tenby is too large for me some days." She felt his gaze on her, thoughtful, palpable. Before sense, or caution, could win over she added. "If I could be mistress of someplace equal to Blackstone Abbey...that would suit me." after a hesitation she glanced over to see his eyes flick away from hers.

Regretting her boldness she nudged her horse into a short gallop ahead of he and her father. Dunsworth brought his horse nearer Lord Riley and Isabel could hear them speaking more of horses, then agriculture.

On their way back to Tenby, passing over a small creek on the other side of which was a small cliff, Isabel looked up to where stood a small gazebo. A memory returned to her of she and Miranda's fifteenth birthday, of tripping into Dunsworths arms like a clutz and then being caught in an almost-embrace by a gaggle of youths. How embarrassed she had been over that incident, even up to earlier this year. Six months ago that event seemed like it had happened so recently. Now it somehow felt that time had sped up, she was a few months away from nineteen and eighteen felt as though it was a decade past.

She did not notice Dunsworth had broken away from her father to speak to her, and when he spoke she ate her heart. "What is it you are staring at so intently? Oh, I frightened you. You must have been very intent indeed, have I interrupted a daydream?"

"It is the other twin that daydreams," grinned she, "not I. I was merely looking at the gazebo yonder and it reminded me of a time something humorous happened...at a birthday party."

"Ah..strange, you know, I also hold a memory of something that occurred in that particular gazebo."

Isabel's heart once more rose to her throat. "Oh?" she managed to squeak. "and what memory is that?"

"Well now, as you have asked, it would be the gentlemanly thing to divulge the tale. Here you have it, I was in that gazebo with a young lady and two others – this was three nigh-on-four years ago – when lo, her companions fled; no doubt conspiring with the lady that she may have me alone for some nefarious purpose, some scheme.."

Isabel listened, catching almost immediately that he was speaking of the same event that had haunted her unnecessarily ever since its fruition. He had bloody remembered. First she listened intrigued, discomfited; then indignantly "Nefarious purpose?! I had no such.." but Dunsworth continued his tale over-top her words, lips twitching with humor.

"I found myself solitary in her presence, defenseless. I insisted we rejoin the others but she would have none of it – she was desperate for my abundant wealth and dashing looks you see – I was most uncommonly handsome in my youth I'll have you know.."

"Oh yes, I imagine you were; whatever happened." Isabel snickered.

"Hush, I'm telling you the story as you asked. The girl then pounced upon me most brazenly, threw herself into my arms; the gall. What say you, Miss Riley, was I not lucky we were then found by a group of partygoers and I given the opportunity to escape?"

"I say, Sir, you are lucky indeed..to have ladies so willing to throw themselves into your arms. You are the envy of every second son."

"It is a burden, yes," sighed he in jest "for the one lady I do love guards her heart so well I cannot tell if my love might be well received."

"It is a pity you did not love the lady in the gazebo; for it seems to me that if it were she you loved, your love would be veritably received." She smiled a little and gazed back at the structure that had sparked their current conversation. Dunsworth merely chortled.

Lord Riley pulled up near them and pointed out a small estate situated some three or four miles behind Tenby.

"Those are close neighbors." Dunsworth commented.

"They would be if it were not vacant. McLoughlin Manor has not been occupied these past fifteen years, or more, if my memory serves me well."

"It seems a tidy estate."

"Not decrepit by any means."

"Why has it not been purchased?"

"Too isolated, I imagine, for anyone who is not friends with one or two families nearby. Most prefer to be nearer towns and cities than we. It is considerably cheaper than it's worth, but that doesn't seem to have enticed anyone as yet. I imagine it will eventually be taken up by an older couple wishing for country air, or by a newly-wed couple who wish for a large estate but have only the funds for a little one." Lord Riley chuckled. "Though the latter is unlikely considering young people are customarily found where there are other young people."

"Customarily." Dunsworth agreed with a smile.

Lord Riley put his fingers to his mouth and caused an ear-splitting whistle to shred the air. Isabel turned in her saddle to see what was about. "Back this way Izzy!" her father called. "We have already been out too long, we did not tell the others we were gone riding, recall; they will wonder where we ran off too!"

~~~
~~~

"You are pleased with Odin? He is not too burdensome a gift?" Isabel asked once they led the beasts to their stalls and returned to the house.

"No gift could have pleased me more. I like him so well I am tempted to ride him all the way home to Blackstone."

"Oh don't, please. That would be too long a journey for this cold, you will catch your death!"

"Very well, for your sake I shall only ride a few miles, after which I shall retreat into the safety of the carriage."

"I am satisfied." grinned she. "I shan't suffer our hospitable reputation to be marred by sending a guest home in discomfort."

"There you are!" Miranda cried from the stairs at the far side of the great hall. "How could you have gone riding without me, Izzy. Fie!"

Chapter 33

The women preferred not to go out hunting the next day. As much as Izzy and Sicily quite enjoyed it on any other day, it was simply too cold out for their tastes and so they chose the less invigorating but equally enjoyable activity of redressing bonnets with new ribbons and florals; the three older ladies having gone up to check that luggage was packed and ready to be brought out once the men had returned.

"That is quite pretty Miss Riley." Sicily leaned over to admire the twins' handiworks. "I never thought of putting silk roses on the underside."

Miranda received the compliment with humble pride.

"How are you meant to wear it?" Isabel questioned, sewing a thick ribbon into pleats around the band of her project.

"I have a picture in my mind of wearing it tipped back and to the side a little, then if I do my hair in a high style the roses with frame it nicely. I saw a woman our age wearing something similar while in London – I thought I might try my hand at re-creating it." She paraded it on her head for her companions to observe.

"Seems a bit impractical, you will have to wear it with very specific styles and outfits." Isabel commented. "But it is very pretty."

"I quite like it!" Sicily reached for it, wishing to try it on herself.

Miranda declared immediately "Why Miss Dunsworth, this is a perfect piece for you! You do not have to try and style your hair around it at all."

"I really wish I could look so handsome with hair so short." Isabel sighed, "but blond hair would not compliment the style I'm sure."

"Heavens no! How could you think of cutting your hair, Izzy! Shocking!" Miranda laughed. "It looks lovely on Miss Dunsworth and suits her personality well, but I would not recommend it for you!"

"I feel blond hair would look very elegant short." Sicily replied, returning Miranda's work to her. "And if Izzy tried it and decided it did not look well on her it would re-gain it's length soon enough."

"Perhaps, but she would receive little attention from potential suitors in the meantime."

Sicily grinned. "Quite the opposite I imagine."

"I don't endeavor to offend, but I do not think men very much inclined towards women who sport manly appearances."

"On the contrary, I have received significant number of proposals despite my cut and style; I am single by choice not due to a lack of offers."

"I hope you know it was not my intent to insult.."

Sicily assured her friend kindly. "I know how you meant it, Miss Riley, I am not offended."

"Did you not care for any of those who asked for your hand?" Miranda then added quickly.

"No...I make friends easily enough, but in my experience men don't seem capable of just being friends with a woman;" she laughed, "they are romantic creatures and always end up falling in love – be it with the woman or her wealth."

"Have you never been in love?"

"Not until recently."

"Why Sicily, how have I not heard of this." Isabel teased. "I thought we were to know everything about one-another!" Miss Dunsworth laughed awkwardly in reply. "Tell us a name, you know we shan't tell a soul!" But Miss Dunsworth would not be persuaded.

"I am sorry, Ladies, that is a name I shall take with me to my grave."

"Surely not! He will fall for you just as everyone does; then we shall know this mystery man!" Isabel stated with certainty.

Miss Dunsworth barked a short laugh. "I'm afraid it is impossible for us to be together; and even if it were not, the person in question told me in confidence, ignorant of my keen affection for them, that they love another. I also know their love is reciprocated and so I will be very content seeing the two mopsy's happy together...now let us please divagate from this topic." added she quietly.

The twins glanced at each other with mutual sorrow on behalf of their heartsick friend, respecting her wishes and lightening the mood with cheerful banter.

~~~

The men returned just after one o'clock, much to everyone's despondency for, not only did they return empty-handed, now they were back it was time for a quick lunch before Tenby's guests would depart. Isabel's anxiety
~~~

increased. As much as she tried to remain prudent and dispassionate, her heart wailed at the thought of Eugene Dunsworth leaving, not knowing when she might see him again; hoping there might be time, still, for him to take her aside and proclaim his undying, staggering love for her. Alas, every minute that sped by frayed that hope until – final embraces and handshakes carried out – the guests lighted into their respective modes of transport (Eugene astride Odin) and were flown away in a breath. Matthew, Lord Riley, and Miranda turned to re-enter the manor.

"Come dearest," Miranda laid a land gently on her twin's shoulder.

~~~

Isabel sat in a window seat in the little library trying to distract herself with an adventure novel; gazing instead out the window upon the courtyard for a full half-hour, deep in thought. Movement caused her eye to drift to the end of the drive. She recognized Odin in an instant, and the rider in the next. "Papa!" cried she, now running to find him. "Papa, Mr Dunsworth returns!"

"Mr Dunsworth? Returning?" Miranda emerged from another room. "He must have forgotten som.... go quickly to meet him, Izzy." She pushed her twin towards the door. "Papa is in his study with Matthew. I shall inform him one of our guests have returned...and shall occupy Matthew elsewhere."

Isabel fled to the front doors. Heart pounding in anticipation even as she told herself to remain rational. Isabel stepped down to the pebbled courtyard just as Eugene Dunsworth slid off his horse and led it towards her.

"You are back!" said she, eagerness lending a slight tremor to her voice. "Have you forgotten something?"

"I..yes."
~~~

There was a very prolonged silence in which neither of them moved, or even ceased gazing at the other.

"I had to return, Miss Riley. I.." he reached for her hand, which she very willingly allowed him to take "I couldn't leave without asking...without telling you I..." He swallowed.

"Without telling me what..?" she encouraged, a little giggle bursting forth before she was able to stop it.

He closed his eyes briefly tight, looking to the sky as he struggled, the corners of his mouth began to twitch upward. "Miss Riley may I.." His eyes met hers once more, unsuccessful in holding back his grin. "Shall I..Miss Riley should I speak to your father? Do I have any hope?.."

"Yes! Oh, absolutely! Yes, he is in his study and very prepared to give us every blessing! Make haste and come straight back to me!"

Dunsworth's grin widened and he left her with Odin to jog into the house. Haste was made indeed, Lord Riley did not linger in giving Eugene Dunsworth a favorable response to his request. The young man fled outdoors once more with uncharacteristic abandon to rejoin his lady, who laughed in joy at seeing him approach. She was wrapped in a tight embrace and lifted high, neither of them able to cease their beaming smiles.

"You must spin me around now for I believe that is the romantic thing to do!" joked she; then shrieked gleefully as he did just so.

~ Epilogue ~

The Riley twins were married together on a warm, though slightly drizzly day, in the summer of 1815.

Matthew and Miranda Westbrook honeymooned in Rome for three weeks, while Eugene and Isabel Dunsworth were content to spend a few days in Bath before returning to their new home.

Isabel was kept ignorant of she and her husband's home, he wanted the first time she saw it to be when he 'carried her through the door'. She lamented a mite too often how desperately she would miss her sister now they were both married and living their separate lives, how far Southamptons was from Tenby, how lonely Papa must be with his girls both gone so suddenly. Eugene eventually commented that if she continued bemoaning such things so often he would begin to think she was having regrets marrying him. He was very quickly convinced otherwise.

The carriage curtains were drawn the full way home after their stay in bath; Isabel was giddy with excitement and anticipation. They finally came to a halt.

"Close your eyes and I will lead you out." Dunsworth instructed with a bit of a smile in his voice.

Isabel obeyed.

"There, you may look."

Isabel Dunsworth stood in shock as she looked upon the manor before her. "Why, Eugene, it is McLoughlin!" She spun around, searching the surrounding hills, pointing exuberantly. "Oh! Oh it is McLoughlin Manor! There is Tenby, and there is Thornhill in the distance!" beginning to shed bright tears against her will she fell into her husband's arms, kissing his cheeks. "I feel all the more guilty for wailing on and on about how I will miss my friends and family. I ruined our honeymoon for naught."

"Not in the least, my dear." reassured he, looking mightily pleased. "It made surprising you all the sweeter."

"I love you!"

"And I, you." Grinned he, lacing his fingers with hers as they walked towards their new home.